MR. APRIL

HEROES OF ROGUE VALLEY: CALENDAR GUYS

BOOK 4

ANN ROTH

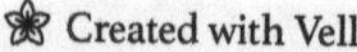 Created with Vellum

INTRODUCTION

Welcome to Ann Roth's exciting new series, Heroes of Rogue Valley: Calendar Guys *series. Twelve months, 12 gorgeous firefighter heroes and the women who steal into their hearts and forever change their lives.*

Meet Mr. April:

When firefighter Owen Ayers lets freelance writer Hallie Sawyer shadow him for her Guff's Lake Fire Department magazine article, what should be an easy task proves challenging instead. Jaded by his failed marriage and wary of getting involved, Owen is irresistibly drawn to Hallie. Shattered after the unimaginable death of her fiancé and the miscarriage that followed, Hallie is slowly rebuilding her life and focusing on her career. But smart, sexy Owen threatens to breach her protective shell. The healing power of love just might save them both.

Mr. April–Owen Ayers
    Age 34, 6' tall, 180 pounds
    Single

Proud Senior Firefighter
Time with Guff's Lake Fire Department: 9 years

At nine on the dot Tuesday morning, Hallie Sawyer strode into the visitors area of the Guff's Lake Fire Department. The sound of her heels clicking across the tile floor made her feel important. Her whole carefully crafted look, from her French twist to her crisp linen blouse, pencil skirt and summer pumps screamed professional magazine writer—she hoped.

So what if she'd spent more on the outfit than her budget allowed? Making an impression mattered. And she so needed this assignment to pan out.

Forcing a confident smile, she approached the thirty-something female seated behind a protective glass barrier. "Hi, Ms. Zindell," she said after a quick glance at the woman's nameplate. "I have an appointment with Captain Comings."

Hallie had contacted Fire Prevention magazine about writing a four-part series profiling fire departments in midsize towns across the country, with Guff's Lake, Oregon, as the launch story. As yet the magazine had contracted for only the Guff's Lake story, but if the article was good enough, surely a series would follow.

Had to, because making her hard-earned money stretch between writing assignments wasn't easy. A little short-term certainty would be nice, and who knew what doors her success might open?

"Everyone calls me Miranda," the receptionist said. She gave Hallie a quizzical look. "Do I know you?"

"I don't believe so. I'm Hallie Sawyer."

Miranda's eyes widened before she offered the sympathetic look Hallie had come to expect and dread. "I remember you from the Guff's Lake News. I'm so sorry."

After four years and umpteen more recent tragedies and distractions, you'd think people would forget. But no. Hallie wished the well-meaning people of Guff's Lake would find someone else to tiptoe around instead. "Thank you," she murmured with barely a stumble.

"I'll let Captain Comings know you're here." Miranda picked up the phone and made the call. "He'll be out shortly—with Owen Ayers," she said, clearly expecting a reaction.

AKA Mr. April in the Guff's Lake Fire Department calendar? Ooh. Covering her surprise, Hallie feigned nonchalance. After all, she was a professional writer. Besides, she already knew Owen. Or had. Sort of. Back in high school.

Along with almost everyone else in town, she owned a copy of the calendar that the fire department sold every year, and not just to gaze at the twelve gorgeous males featured—one each month. Proceeds from calendar sales went to the department's benefit fund, which provided assistance to those who needed it after a fire.

Although Hallie had lived in Guff's Lake all her

life, she'd never set foot inside the fire department. "Do you mind if I take pictures of your lobby?" she asked.

"Be my guest."

She wandered around the visitors area, which was filled with photos and memorabilia. A 1913 fire engine from when the department had first opened made for an eye-catching centerpiece. She snapped photos with her cell phone camera and jotted down notes. And wondered about Owen and seeing him in person after all these years... What would that be like?

As she admired the black and white photos from days gone by, the captain and Owen entered the area. She didn't need the calendar to recognize Owen— even if she hadn't seen him since the end of her freshman year in high school. She'd read about his wedding in the paper and later about his divorce, but otherwise had lost track of him.

Neither her memories nor his calendar photo did him justice. Unbelievably, he was even more striking in person than he had been in high school—tall and muscled, with a buzz cut and a strong chin.

A handsome male in his own right, the forty-something captain extended his arm. "Hello, Ms. Sawyer. I'm Captain Comings."

"Please, call me Hallie," she said, smiling as she shook his hand.

"All right. Hallie, this is Owen Ayers—the fire-fighter I've assigned to show you around and answer any questions while you're here."

Hallie and Owen shook hands. His warm, firm grasp dwarfed hers and conveyed confidence. The magnetic eyes no sane woman could forget, a little close together and a startling navy blue, held her gaze and brought back the fluttery feeling she'd had in high school.

"Weren't you in Pearl's class at Orchard High?" he asked.

He remembered? "That's right. Freshman year, we played on the girls' JV soccer team together and became friends. You were on the boys' varsity basketball team."

"That was a long time ago."

"Fifteen years." But Hallie hadn't forgotten. From the second she'd laid eyes on Owen Ayers, she'd been smitten with the biggest crush...

Four years older and a senior, he'd never paid her any attention. Why would he? She'd been skinny and straight as a stick, with a mouth full of braces. Besides, all his focus had been on beautiful Colleen, his steady girlfriend and now ex-wife.

"Let's go into the training room and talk," Captain Comings said. He entered a code into a keypad on a locked door. When the latch clicked open, he gestured Hallie through.

With the distinct feeling the two men were assessing her from the back, she straightened her shoulders and entered the interior of the fire department.

OWEN WASN'T THRILLED about being shadowed for two days, but he could do a lot worse than spend a few days showing Hallie Sawyer around, he thought as he and the captain flanked her on the way to the training room. She was attractive. About five feet seven and curvy. Tawny skin, big eyes, dark brown hair pulled back into something fancy. Great legs, too, at least from what he could see in her knee-length skirt.

She looked a whole lot different from when the Rogue Valley News and online reporters had plastered photos of her everywhere during the weeks following the tragedy.

Surely he would have remembered the teenage version of her. He didn't. He could only recall that she and his sister Pearl had hung out in high school. He'd been too wrapped up in Colleen and his own life to pay attention to his sister's friends. He made a mental note to look Hallie up in the yearbook—if he could find it. No doubt, Pearl had held onto her copy.

The stuff he knew about Hallie was more recent. For months, her agonizing story had haunted him and everyone else in town. A member of the well-known and respected Sawyer Construction family, pregnant and soon to be married, she had had everything to look forward to, and life had looked bright and promising. Until the fateful evening Simon Wharton, her fiancé, had stopped at a convenience store to pick up a fresh supply of the beef jerky she craved during her pregnancy.

Minutes later, two thugs high on meth and intent on robbing the store had entered the building. In a classic holdup-gone-bad, Simon had been shot and killed, his only mistake being in the wrong place at the wrong time.

Owen and his eleven crewmates had been off-duty that night, but the story had quickly spread through the entire department and the whole of Guff's Lake.

If that wasn't horrendous enough, shortly after the funeral Hallie had miscarried.

Compared to her losses, his sob story seemed trivial.

The captain gestured Hallie to take a seat at the table the station used for group trainings. Owen sat next to him, across from her. The table was wide, and about seven feet separated them. Even so, he could smell her perfume. Something subtle and sweet. Lilacs—a breath of spring in the scorching summer. Nice mouth, too. Her generous lips looked soft and inviting.

But he wasn't here to think about that.

"At the Guff's Lake Fire Department, our crews work two back-to-back, twenty-four-hour shifts per week," Captain Comings began. "This crew works Mondays and Tuesdays."

Her head bent toward her note pad, she scribbled furiously while her mouth formed an intriguing O.

The captain nodded for Owen to take over.

"As Captain Comings mentioned, I'll be showing you the ropes and answering any questions while you shadow me."

She looked up, her eyes lit with excitement. "I get to shadow you for forty-eight hours straight?"

Owen couldn't believe she'd asked.

The captain appeared equally flabbergasted. "That won't be possible. You're welcome here between seven-thirty and eighteen hundred hours—we use military time. Our morning meeting begins at zero eight hundred sharp. Owen will give you a copy of our Ride Along Policy. Read it before you come back."

Owen slid the paper across the table to her. "When will your article be published?"

"It's scheduled for the November issue of Fire Prevention magazine. As soon as I get copies, I'll send one to the department."

"We'll look forward to reading it," the captain said. While she put the ride-along rules in her notes folio he nodded at Owen and stood. "I'll leave you two to work out the details.

"You wouldn't want to sleep here even for one night," Owen said after his boss left. "Sometimes we're so busy we don't rest much."

"But I'd get a real feel for what you experience in forty-eight hours."

His head filled with all sorts of interesting late-night images, none of them having to do with his job. He cleared his throat. "You'll learn plenty during the day. Besides, there's no place for you to bunk."

Hallie nodded. "Why don't you employ any female firefighters here?"

"We'd like to, but so far it hasn't worked out."

"Why not?"

"This is a physically difficult job and extremely competitive. For every job opening we post, we get upward of two thousand applications. Most are from men, but occasionally a woman applies."

"What do you do on a twenty-four-hour shift?"

"I'll show you Monday. Our shift officially begins with a meeting at zero eight hundred, but if I were you, I'd arrive at seven-thirty and join us for breakfast. Ditto with lunch, which is at twelve hundred. Both are BYOF—bring your own food. Your day here ends when we sit down to dinner."

"Okay. Do you bring your own dinner, too?"

Owen shook his head. "We take turns providing and cooking the evening meal."

"Is it okay to take photos for the article?"

She sure was full of questions. "You'll have to clear that with the captain. Punctuality is important, so be on time. One more thing, which you'll read about when you look over the Ride-Along Policy. Dress conservatively and neatly in dark pants and a shirt. No sandals or heels." Wanting to return to the job, he checked his watch.

"You probably need to get back to work." Hallie slid her folio into a large shoulder bag and stood. "Thanks for giving me this opportunity."

"My pleasure." Before he could stop himself, his gaze swept over her.

Damn, he liked what he saw. He opened the door to the lobby and ushered her through.

2

The second Owen walked into his house Friday evening, Opal made a beeline for him. "You were gone a long time, Uncle Owen! I'm hungry."

Grinning, he ruffled her hair. And look at that, he was playing the family man he'd always wanted to be. She was his niece, not his kid, and this was temporary, but he sure was crazy about her. Having her and Pearl bunking with him had definitely altered his life as a single man.

"Hi there, graham cracker," he said, using the nickname borne from her love for the crackers. "It's Friday night and Mama's Cantina was packed, but I got it." He held up the fragrant bag of steaming food.

Standing nearby, Pearl licked her lips. "That sure smells good."

Pain shadowed her eyes. By this time of day, her back often bothered her. Four months ago, as she drove to her new admin job at the hospital, her world had tilted sideways. A head-on collision with a drunk driver had put a hold on her employment and left her with a totaled car and substantial injuries.

The drunken woman who'd hit her carried no insurance and was now in jail. Pearl's seatbelt had saved her from head trauma, and her auto insurance had paid out enough for her to buy a decent used vehicle. But she'd sustained a fractured back that had required surgery and several months for her to recuperate.

In limbo on health insurance, which kicked in ninety days after she started her job, and saddled with staggering medical bills, she'd soon lost her apartment. Owen had moved her and his niece into his three-bedroom home.

He touched Pearl's shoulder. "Why don't you lie down?"

"I'm okay," she insisted. "Opal, please wash up, then help your uncle Owen set the table."

"Maybe you should take a pain pill," he said after the little girl skipped toward the powder room.

His sister shook her head. "I'll put the heating pad on after dinner."

"If you overdo the physical therapy, your back will take longer to heal completely," he warned.

"I'm not pushing myself that hard. Now that the doctor cleared me to start work the week after next, I need to be extra strong so that I can put in forty hours a week. Then I can quit sponging off you."

Thanks to growing up with parents who had divorced each other twice, remarried each other three times and burdened themselves with perpetual debt, neither Owen nor his sister liked borrowing or owing money to anyone, including family.

The accident had changed that. "You'd do the same for me," he said. "You'll be independent in no time."

"The sooner, the better. I'm going to start paying you back as soon as I get my first paycheck. I have it all budgeted out."

Having covered her staggering medical bills and

the physical therapy, Owen doubted she'd ever be able to fully repay him. He didn't begrudge her, was grateful he'd had the funds to help her out. Only now, his once-fat savings account was all but drained—not a comfortable place to be.

"Your first priority is an apartment for you and Opal," he said. "Hey, do you remember Hallie Sawyer?"

Pearl smiled. "Of course. We had some good times in high school. Then we lost touch—although I did send her a card after she lost her fiancé and the baby. So sad. Why do you ask?"

"She's writing an article about the fire department and will be shadowing me next week."

The more he thought about seeing her again, the more he looked forward to it. Not that he'd ever admit it. His assignment was to show her the ropes, period.

"Small world. I'd love to see her. Tell her 'Hi,' and give her my number."

"Will do. I don't remember her from high school, and I can't find my yearbook."

"Look through mine. It's in my closet, in a box labeled, 'Yearbooks.' "

Opal was busy doing whatever a five-year-old girl did in the bathroom. While waiting for her, Owen brought the box into the kitchen. He found the right year and located Hallie's photos—there were several, none bearing a likeness to her now. In those pictures, she had gangly arms and legs, braces on her teeth, and no curves. She sure had changed. "I still don't remember her," he said.

"Don't tell her that. I think she had a crush on you."

"No kidding." He filed that interesting tidbit away for later.

At last, Opal returned to help Owen with the table.

"I keep meaning to tell you—Adam is going propose to Sam tonight," he told Pearl over the meal.

"Wonderful! She'll say yes, right?"

"You know it. They're solid."

"Adam's a good man. Sam's lucky. So is he."

"Some people are," Owen agreed.

His sister gave him a telling look. As in, Not you and me.

Divorce was in their genes, or so their dad claimed. The only family members in a lasting marriage were Owen and Pearl's maternal grandparents. Fifty years together and they were still going strong.

At one time Owen had believed he'd beat the odds, that he and Colleen would follow in their footsteps. He'd been wrong. Two years after the divorce, he was easing back into dating, but keeping things light. He didn't want to get tangled up in anything serious, wasn't sure he ever would. Colleen had done a number on him. She—

"Uncle Owen, I said, what does 'solid' mean?" Opal asked.

"It means Adam and Sam are a good couple and that their relationship will last."

Opal chattered away, full of talk about starting kindergarten in two weeks. Earlier today Owen's grandma had bought her a new outfit and shoes for school, and she could hardly wait to wear them. Then she switched gears. "After dinner, can we watch Frozen?"

"Go ahead, but I have to pass," he said. "I need to work."

He'd have preferred to hang out with her or better yet, play poker with his teammates at their standing Friday night game. Unfortunately, he was too deep into the weeds with revamping the fire safety training program he'd originally brought to market three years ago.

Fire departments that had bought the first version were clamoring for an updated one. New clients also wanted it and were willing to pay top dollar. Orders had flooded in, which was great. The money Owen earned would replenish his bank account.

But the programming changes and sheer volume of the material made progress slow-going and frustrating. Owen had exactly three weeks to finish the thing and send it to his beta testers. They needed a few days to run through it and report any glitches. And there were always glitches. Owen figured he'd need an additional week to fix them.

"But you worked all day," Opal whined.

True that. Since his shift at the station had ended, he'd been at it continually—even pulling a couple all-nighters.

Pearl shook her head. "If it weren't for my accident, you'd be done with that program by now."

"That has nothing to do with my slow progress. Besides, you know how much I enjoy tinkering."

"My brother, the geek."

"You'd better believe it."

"What's a geek?" Opal asked.

"A person who likes computers and math and technical stuff," Owen replied. He'd been fascinated with all three since high school. Not enough to make a full-time career of it. First and foremost, he was a firefighter.

"I like computers, too."

He chuckled. "My little geek in training."

"Please, please don't work tonight, Uncle Owen."

"I have to, graham cracker."

She looked disappointed. "Tell you what," he said.

"After dinner tomorrow, I'll take you and your mom out for ice cream cones."

"Can I get bubble-gum flavor and sprinkles?"

"Sprinkles, too? You drive a hard bargain, but okay."

His niece brightened right up.

Score one for Uncle Owen. If only all life's problems were as easy to solve.

SUNDAY AFTERNOON HALLIE pulled up the winding, mile-long private road that wound through the ten-acre plot of land her paternal grandfather had purchased long before her parents had met. Except for Hallie, the entire Sawyer clan lived on the premises, each family in a custom home on an acre of land.

Her undeveloped acre stood waiting for her to build a house and move in. She had no plans to do so, and with good reason. Her parents and grandparents tended to smother her—as if she needed watching over. Hallie was determined to prove she didn't need them.

Aside from that, building a house cost money she didn't have and refused to borrow—even if she could qualify for a loan, which she couldn't. Then there was the implied assumption that the property had been set aside for when she married and had kids.

Who knew when or if she'd fall in love again, let alone get married? At the moment she wasn't interested in either. Maybe someday. But pregnancy? The risks alone made her want to throw up.

In no mood to go there, she lowered the Mazda's window and pulled in a breath of air scented with clover and grass—and got smacked with hot air. The window went back up and she enjoyed the view in relative comfort. The Siskiyou Mountains in the distance seemed to glow with rosy color, courtesy of the slanting August sun. The rolling fields on both sides of the road rippled in the gentle breeze. They looked ready for cooler autumn days and much-needed rain. Even the shade trees looked dusty.

Hallie felt dusty, too. After four years, the agony of losing Simon and their unborn daughter had eased to a bearable ache. To the point that lately, she'd begun to miss the feel of a man's arms around her.

She also missed sex. But she'd never been one to jump into bed right away then move on to the next guy. Since she wasn't even dating... Sex would have to wait.

Her closest friend, Paige, whom she'd met at a Living with Loss class several years ago, suggested Hallie consider trying the casual route. Hallie wasn't that desperate. As for Paige, she'd done the opposite and recently remarried.

Hallie's wayward thoughts flashed to Owen Ayers. She'd been drooling over him since Tuesday. His enticing gaze, confident smile, and fit body—talk about heart-thuddingly attractive...

And she called herself a professional writer? A real professional did not sigh dreamily over the man assigned to help her. Frowning, she banished Owen and all his sexiness from her thoughts.

"We're almost there," she told Wilbur, her three-year-old golden lab, who'd been with her since she'd rescued him from the pound as a pup.

Straining against his travel harness in the back seat, he woofed in agreement. Or maybe he was just excited about the visit ahead. "Before we arrive, I want you to know that I will have a good time tonight."

No matter how much her parents pressured her to return to work at Sawyer Construction and move back in with them. As if she were a child instead of a thirty-year-old woman. It happened every time she saw or spoke to them on the phone.

With the approval of the Fire Prevention magazine article and a potential series in sight, she hoped to put a dent in the nagging, at least for a little while.

Yet as excited as she was to talk about her latest writing assignment, timing was everything. She would wait until the right moment.

Through a gap in a bank of poplars she glimpsed Gran and Grandpa's painted white-brick house. Around the next bend the "big house," where her parents lived, with swings, jungle gym, sandbox and trampoline occupying a large section of their ginormous back yard. A spacious patio, manicured lawn and shade trees filled the rest. Along the perimeter were vegetable and flower gardens shared by the whole clan.

Heedless of the sweltering heat, five of Hallie's seven nieces and nephews, ranging in age from four to eight, chased each other across the yard, just as she and her siblings once had. At their heels, three family canines, tongues hanging out, wagged their tails.

Ava and Jimmy, too little to keep up, toddled way behind, and Hallie's younger sister, Libby, and their sisters-in-law lagged even further back. The men were no doubt conferring over the grill.

Hallie honked and parked near the other vehicles in the driveway. Wilbur barked happily and begged to join his friends. She let him out, and he bounded to greet his dog pals and their humans. Thanks to a seven-foot fence around the compound, dogs and kids ran free.

Changing their trajectory, her nieces and nephews raced toward her. "Aunt Hallie! Aunt Hallie!"

Their unfettered joy at seeing her brought out her smile as she bent down and hugged each squirming body. After petting the dogs, she greeted Libby and her sisters-in-law. "I smell steaks," she said, her mouth watering.

"And they're almost ready," replied Libby, a close friend as well as a sister. People said they could pass for twins, probably because they'd both inherited their mother's tawny skin tone, dark, super-curly hair and light-brown eyes. For that matter, so had their brothers, Brett and Joe.

"Mom and the kids made huckleberry ice cream for dessert," Libby added.

"We got to taste some!" Reese, Libby's seven-year-old, announced.

Hallie grinned. "Lucky you. Did you save any for me?"

Angela, one of the sisters-in-law, laughed. "They made gallons of the stuff, and Noreen, Libby, and I baked butter cookies."

The other sister-in-law, Noreen, winked and lowered her voice. "We did our own taste-testing."

At times like this, Hallie felt a little left out. Not that they wouldn't include her if she asked. Sometimes she did, and she always enjoyed herself. But she'd chosen to move away to separate a bit from her family.

"Where are Mom and Gran?" she asked.

"Inside, working on dinner. They kicked us all out," Libby said. "Too noisy, and too many cooks spoiling the broth. But I know they'll want you in there."

As if the two older women somehow heard their

names mentioned, they opened the kitchen door and stepped into the heat to greet Hallie.

Her grandmother, who was too active and energetic to be seventy-six, strode toward her with her arms open for a warm hug. The familiar minty scent she favored filled Hallie's nostrils.

"I made a pitcher of lavender-flavor lemonade just for you," she said.

"My favorite. You spoil me, Gran."

"And I love doing it. Kids, go ask Grandpa when the steaks will be ready. Moms, make sure someone reports back. You come on inside, Hallie."

"What did I tell you?" Libby murmured, her lips twitching. "See you in a few."

Hallie followed her mother and grandmother into the cool, spacious kitchen. Thirsty, she poured herself a glass of lemonade. Because it was too hot to eat outside, she arranged place mats on the large, round kitchen table.

"I'm so happy you're here," her mother said, as if Hallie had been gone for weeks instead of a few days. "I wish we saw more of you."

And the nagging had started. Couldn't she leave it alone, just once?

Hallie fought the urge to snap at her, but remembering her vow to enjoy the evening, she kept a pleasant expression on her face and an easy tone. "I'm here every Sunday, Mom, and we talk a couple times a week."

"Yes, but you live way out in the boonies, a thirty-minute drive one way. Who has time to drop by on a whim? If you moved back home, we could see you every day."

Have the family poking their noses into her business any old time? No, thanks. That part of her life was over and done with. "I'm happy living out there."

The rent was cheap and the nearest neighbors lived far enough away that Hallie finally had the privacy she'd always craved.

"All by yourself." Gran shook her head. "That sounds so lonely."

At times, but for the most part, Hallie reveled in the peace and quiet. "Actually, I enjoy the solitude," she repeated for what seemed the dozenth time.

"I don't understand how you—"

To Hallie's relief, the door opened and Libby poked her head inside. "The steaks will be ready in five minutes. The kids are coming in to wash up."

Hallie's nieces and nephews and their mothers streamed into the kitchen. Behind them, her grandfather and father. Last but definitely not least, her brothers and brother-in-law, each carrying a platter of mouthwatering T-bones. Enough to feed an army, but then the eighteen members of the extended Sawyer family were about the size of a small army.

While Hallie exchanged hugs and greetings with the men, Noreen herded the older kids to the powder room to wash up. Libby and Angela escorted their toddlers to another bathroom to change diapers.

Hallie, her mother, and Gran set pitchers and side dishes on the lazy Susan at the center of the table. In no time the whole family sat down and helped themselves. Dinner was loud, chaotic and utterly wonderful.

But at the end of the meal, that changed.

3

___

Not long after Hallie's extended family finished dinner, the kids raced outside to take advantage of the fading daylight. Gran and Grandpa accompanied them to keep an eye on the little ones, leaving the remaining family to linger over decaf coffees.

With everyone full and relaxed, this seemed the perfect time for Hallie to talk about her new assignment. "I had a meeting at the fire department this week," she began.

Libby nodded. "You mentioned that awhile back. How did it go?"

"Very well. The captain gave his okay for me to write an article for Fire Prevention magazine. Now for the cool part." Leaning forward, Hallie grinned. "Next week I get to shadow a firefighter."

Referring to Owen simply as a firefighter—nice touch. She gave herself a mental pat on the back.

"What exactly will that entail?" her father asked. His eyes narrowed a fraction, which could mean anything.

At fifty-eight, his once light-brown hair had grayed and begun to thin, and years of working outdoors had given him a permanently weathered look. But he remained as sharp and opinionated as ever.

"From what I understand, I'll follow the man around and learn first-hand how he and the rest of the crew fill their day," she said. "I plan to take tons of pictures and ask lots of questions."

Looking impressed, her older brother, Brett rested on his forearms. "Cool."

Joe, the oldest sibling, gave an approving nod. "If I weren't in construction, I'd be a firefighter."

Hallie hadn't heard that before, but then her parents and grandparents expected family members to join Sawyer Construction. She'd followed along, working there part time after high school and college before going full time. After life had thrown its brutal curveball four years ago, she'd changed course and left the company—the first and only Sawyer to break with tradition.

Joe's wife, Noreen, also seemed surprised. "You love your job."

"You know it, but way back when, I used to dream of joining the fire department."

"According to Owen, landing a job as a firefighter is very competitive," Hallie said.

Her mother frowned. "Who's Owen?"

"The man I'll be shadowing." Hallie was pleased at her tone, which indicated professional interest only.

"Owen Ayers—Mr. April? Wow." Libby glanced at the Guff's Lake Fire Department calendar hanging on the wall near the back door. This was August and Owen's photo was no longer displayed, but she obviously remembered him.

What red-blooded female wouldn't? More than once while salivating over his photo the entire month of April, Hallie had imagined him undressed. She'd bet her laptop they had, too.

Libby blew her husband a kiss. "Don't worry, Chase, you're the only man for me."

Noreen and Brett's wife, Angela, both let out sighs, then nodded at their husbands. "Ditto for us."

"That's one reason I wanted to be a firefighter—women go for those guys." Joe gave a cockeyed grin.

Brett looked thoughtful. "I knew Owen in high school. We were in the same history class. Back then he was a computer nerd and a varsity basketball player. A brainy athlete. I guess that's how he got foxy Colleen Graves to go steady with him. They got married right out of high school. Now they're divorced."

"It wasn't just brains and athletic ability. He was also good-looking," Hallie said. Now that he'd filled out and matured, the man was off-the-charts gorgeous. "His sister, Pearl, and I used to hang out together."

"I remember that," her mom said. She and Hallie's dad aimed speculative looks Hallie's way. "Is Owen single now?"

Hallie wondered the same thing. She shrugged. "I don't know and I don't care. My focus will be on gathering information for my article." Period. No daydreaming allowed.

"I know, honey. I just think it'd be nice if you started dating again."

Hallie wasn't ready by a long shot. Now her eyes narrowed. "Don't, Mom."

"Your mother only wants you to be happy," her dad said. "We all do."

Everyone at the table nodded.

"I am happy," she insisted. Most of the time. "I love my work."

Writing magazine articles freelance had become her whole life. The work was satisfying, never boring, and kept her busy. Yes, the pay sucked, but peace of mind was more important than making money. Besides, as her portfolio of writing credits grew, she had no doubt she'd eventually earn a steady stream of income. Who knew, she might even land a full-time writing job.

Her mom frowned. "Shadowing a firefighter sounds dangerous."

"She'll be fine," Brett said.

Joe echoed the sentiment.

"Have a little faith, Mom." Hallie thought about the ride-along document she'd read. "The department won't allow me to put myself in harm's way. Anyway, it's only for two days."

"Two days?" Joe echoed.

"In Guff's Lake, the firefighters work two back-to-back, twenty-four-hour shifts. I'll be there during the day."

"Accidents happen," her mother persisted. "You could get hurt. I don't understand why you need to do this, Hallie."

Hallie's temper stirred. "Shadow a firefighter or write articles for a living?"

"Lay off, Mom," Joe warned.

She didn't argue, instead homed in on Hallie's father. "Tell her, Jim."

He nodded, and just like that the pressure was on full tilt. "During the five years you managed our office after college, you did a crackerjack job," he said. "Everyone liked you and the office never ran smoother. Even Judy says so."

"And you know how wonderful she was when she

retired and trained you for the job," Hallie's mom chimed in.

And back to Dad. "When you had your, ah, setback, she came out of retirement and took the job back so that you could heal. She'll be seventy soon, and she's ready to retire for good. It's time you rejoined the company."

"I lost the love of my life, Dad, and our unborn daughter. That's a whole lot more than a 'setback.'"

Everyone had gone still, as if they feared Hallie was so fragile, she'd break apart at the mere mention of her devastating losses. When it'd been almost two years since she'd fallen apart like that.

Couldn't they see how strong she'd grown? Frustrated and angry, she stiffened. Caught herself and with effort, stuffed her temper back inside.

"I know I did a good job, Dad," she said in her most reasonable voice. "But as proud as I am of my work there and as much as I respect and admire the family company, I need to be out on my own."

Her mother scoffed. "No, you need your family, including Sawyer Construction. What's wrong with letting us be here for you?"

Thanks for hearing me, Mom. "You know I love and appreciate you all, and I'm beyond grateful for your support. I couldn't have survived these past four years without you. But I'm not an office manager anymore. I'm a writer."

"Earning peanuts when you could be making a good salary with benefits. I don't see how you—"

Hallie snapped. "Stop it, Mom!"

Collective sharp intakes of breath all around. Her mother looked startled. "Now, don't get upset, honey."

"Then quit nagging me." Hallie exhaled and tried again. "Look, Brett, Joe, and Chase are at the company, and Libby, Angela, and Noreen work part time because they're raising kids. I don't see what difference it makes if I'm not there."

Her father's face reddened and he clamped his jaw, a sign that he was as angry as Hallie. "We want you back. I don't know how else to say it. I'm not offering you a cushy job on a silver platter, Hallie. You'll work hard for your salary just as you did before, and be well-compensated. At least then you'll be able to afford to move into a decent house until you're ready to build your own right here."

Hallie opened her mouth, then shut it. Why even bother arguing? Her parents refused to listen and never would.

Resigned and weary, she sighed. "We all have to work tomorrow. I should leave soon. Mom and Dad, why don't you go outside with Gran, Grandpa, and the kids, and let the rest of us clean up this dinner mess. I'll come out and say good night before I go."

She stood and began clearing the table.

~

ALTHOUGH BREAKFAST at the station wasn't mandatory Monday morning, Owen had never missed a single one. Vacations and illness aside, neither had anyone else on the team. By the time he picked up his food at Rosemary's Breakfast Nook, conveniently located only blocks from the station, stowed his gear and sat down at the dining table, the captain and most of the crew had already assembled for the meal.

Adam arrived last. In Guff's Lake, news spread like wildfire, and everyone knew Sam had accepted his proposal.

Rafe got off the first gibe. "If it isn't Mr. Bites the Dust."

A volley of good-natured teasing followed, which Adam tolerated for a while before firing back at Rafe. "You're one to talk. You're next."

That seemed likely, and the man formerly known as the stud of the station didn't argue.

"Have you set a date for the big day?" Captain Comings asked.

"We have—next April. Get out your phones and mark your calendars." Adam shared the date.

Rafe frowned. "That's about eight months from now. Why wait?"

"We're waiting until after I formally adopt William." Sam's almost six-year-old son. "That should be finalized in a couple of months, but by then it'll be cold and the mountain passes could be tricky for Sam's parents to cross."

"Makes sense," Gus commented. "Sam asked Wanda to do her hair."

Gus was the latest to hook up with a woman perfect for him.

Wedding talk continued, but Owen only listened with half an ear. Any minute, Hallie would be here, and he was way too eager to see her again. He needed to cool it.

He'd just finished his second bacon and egg sandwich when Miranda made an announcement over the PA.

"Owen, Hallie is here."

Seven-thirty on the nose. Owen disposed of his trash and hastened downstairs. He found her in the lobby, chatting with Miranda. She wore her hair in the same fancy twist as before, but she'd dressed appropriately in a modest short-sleeve blouse that draped softly over her breasts, dark slacks, and sneakers.

Coupled with her palpable excitement, she looked good. Real good.

"Hi," he said.

"Good morning." Like the other day, she extended her hand.

Her skin was soft and cool, and her fine-boned fingers felt small and delicate. He wanted to hold on. Did. Her big eyes, a pretty golden brown, widened slightly.

Thanks to going awhile without sex, a certain part of his body took more notice than usual. Dismissing the unwanted heat—he had a job to do, and thinking about anything else was inappropriate—he let go and stepped back. "I mentioned your name to Pearl. She asked me to give you her number."

Hallie looked pleased. "I haven't seen her ages, and I'd love to catch up. What's she up to?"

"She's had a rough four months—fractured her back in a car accident. She hasn't been able to work, so she and Opal are staying with me for a while."

"I'm sorry to hear that. She must be divorced."

Owen nodded.

"I'm guessing Opal is her daughter."

"That's right. She's five, and already knows how to pull my strings."

"A little girl—how lovely." A longing look crossed Hallie's face.

Didn't take a rocket scientist to know she was thinking about the unborn child she'd lost. Owen shoved his hands in his pants pockets and cleared his throat. "I made you sad. I'm awful sorry about Simon and what happened to you."

"Thank you." She dipped her head for a moment. "It's been a hard road, but I'm doing all right. And please, never apologize for mentioning your niece or any other child. I love kids, and with three nieces and four nephews, I'm used to seeing and talking about them. They make me laugh." She dug her cell phone from her purse. "I'm ready for Pearl's number."

She sure had a great attitude. Owen shared his sister's info, then entered the code into the security door and ushered her inside. "Did you bring your breakfast?" he asked as they moved toward the stairs. Hallie nodded and he went on. "The kitchen and eating area are on the second floor. After you eat, I'll show you where to stow your stuff."

He followed her up the steps, his eyes on her backside. Rounded hips and a great ass—she looked as good in slacks as she did in a skirt.

In the kitchen his curious buds, having finished their meal, lingered, every one of them checking her out. Hell, they were guys, but their appreciative looks didn't sit well with Owen. Never mind that he'd done the same thing.

Captain Comings greeted her, then turned to the crew. "This is Hallie Sawyer. She'll be with us today and tomorrow, joining us for breakfast and lunch, as well as attending our daily morning meeting and whatever else comes up. Sit down and eat, Hallie, while we go around the table and introduce ourselves."

Instead of eating, she bit her lip and fidgeted as if nervous. But then she was surrounded by thirteen big men, most of them strangers to her. Owen caught her eye and offered an encouraging smile.

When the crew finished, the captain nodded his

chin Adam's way. "Adam forgot to mention he got engaged over the weekend."

Hallie's eyes widened. "Congratulations. I really like Samantha."

Adam flashed his teeth. "You know her?"

"From a knitting class we took together, about the time you two started dating."

"Cool."

The captain checked his watch. "Owen will field most of Hallie's questions, but I expect the rest of you to be available if needed. See you downstairs at eight hundred hours."

He left. Owen's crewmates came over to greet her personally. To a man they towered over her. Some women would feel overwhelmed, but Hallie had lost what nervousness she'd arrived with. She smiled and shook every hand, clearly impressing the hell out of them—Owen included. Before long, they tromped out of the room and he was alone with her.

"Everyone seems so nice," she said.

"They're the best—like brothers to me."

She nodded. "As I recall, Pearl is your only sibling."

"How do you know that?"

"She told me once. I happen to have two older brothers and a younger sister, and they're also the best. My brother, Brett, mentioned that you were in the same history class."

Owen remembered him. "Smart, about my height —good man."

"I'll tell him you said so."

Hallie's bright smile dazzled him. She sure was pretty, and he was way too interested.

Inappropriate. Starting now, he would work on hiding his attraction. All business again, he gave a terse nod at a jar of markers on a nearby shelf. "Write your name on your lunch and find a place for it in the fridge. We'll stop by your locker on the way to the meeting."

Matching his demeanor, she replied with a solemn nod of her own. He missed that smile, but sticking to the matters at hand was for the best.

4

"I get my own locker?" Hallie asked, impressed that the firefighter department had made room for her.

"Yep. Yours is number fourteen." Owen handed her a lock and the combination. "Stow your stuff. Then we'll head downstairs."

Hallie opened the locker and frowned at the orange vest hanging on the hook. "I think someone else is using this one."

"Nope, it's all yours. That's your safety vest."

She pulled it out and held it up. The word "Observer" was printed in large block letters across the back. "When am I supposed to wear this?"

"Whenever you leave the station, even if you're just stepping out for air. While you shadow me, you're considered a representative of the Guff's Lake Fire Department. That vest looks way too big for you. You need a smaller size."

Owen made a quick call on his cell phone. "Miranda will bring it to the apparatus bay—the garage—where we keep our vehicles and hold our morning meeting."

Hallie could hardly wait. She glanced down at herself. "Is this outfit okay?"

His dark blue eyes flitted down her body. "You look great."

As a thirty-year-old woman, she was used to men looking her over. What surprised her was her own visceral response—the accelerating pulse and flood of heat she was unprepared for. Even if she had fantasized about Owen.

I'm a professional writer, here to learn everything possible about the Guff's Lake Fire Department— nothing more, she reminded herself.

She clutched the vest, a shield of sorts, to her chest.

Owen's attention moved to her shoulder bag. "That thing could hold a horse. What's in there?"

"My notebook and camera, and the usual purse things."

"Purse things—right." Mouth quirking, he glanced at his watch. "We have roughly two minutes until the meeting. Give me the vest, grab what you need, and let's go."

Hallie extracted the notebook, camera, and her cell phone, then squeezed her purse into the locker and spun the lock.

As he hustled her to a different set of stairs at the rear of the building, she noted a brass pole attached from the ceiling and extending down to the lower level. "I had no idea poles like this still existed," she murmured in wonder. "Do I have time to snap a photo?"

"Later."

She'd never been a fan of heights. "Sliding down there on that skinny little thing must be both fun and scary."

Owen chuckled, the nicest sound. "I've never heard it described quite that way."

He was close enough that she smelled his spicy aftershave. Yum. Her stomach flip-flopped. Exasperated with herself, she slid her gel pen into her notebook.

"This pole is used only for fire calls," Owen said. "Otherwise we take the stairs. We'll talk more about that later."

By the time they entered the apparatus bay, the rest of the crew had gathered around the captain. Hallie had barely a moment to take in the sheer size of the place and the multiple fire engines and aid cars.

"Should I stay out of the way?" she asked in a low voice.

"Stand with us." Owen touched the small of her back and guided her forward.

He was being polite, but the touch seemed oddly intimate. Hallie felt warm clear to her toes.

What was the matter with her?

She opened her notebook, pulled the cap off her pen. The captain shared goals for the group as a whole and then addressed each person individually, assigning new projects to some and asking for updates from others. Hallie found out that the firefighters were also certified paramedics and that crew members rotated on a monthly basis between firefighting and paramedic duties. Last on the list were Owen and Hank, a long, lean, solemn-faced man.

"School begins in two weeks," the captain said. "Owen, you're scheduled to teach a basic fire safety workshop for teachers tomorrow morning at the Guff's Lake Community Center. As a follow-up over the next few months, you and Hank will divvy up the schools in Guff's Lake and hold safety training assemblies for kids in each grade level. Hank, you're in charge of the scheduling."

Firefighting entailed much more than Hallie had ever realized, and her mind whirled with all she'd learned. "Am I supposed to go with you to teach that class tomorrow?" she asked after the meeting.

"You're shadowing me and training is part of the job, so yes. Come on, I'll show you around the garage."

While the rest of the crew did what firefighters do in apparatus bays, Owen pointed out special features of each vehicle. Hallie peered inside them all, snapped numerous photos, and took copious notes.

He stopped beside a large fire engine. "One of my duties is to inspect axes and hoses to ensure we're ready for the next call."

As he performed his tasks he explained what he was doing and answered all her questions. Watching him work was sheer pleasure. He certainly had broad shoulders. His shirt strained across them as he expertly recoiled a hose.

Was it any wonder she was attracted to him?

"This apparatus bay is spotless," she said. "No dirt, litter, or oil spots. I could probably eat off it."

Owen's lips twitched. "You don't want to do that. Around here, we keep things neat and orderly. It's part of the job."

"Except for the stuff on the floor." Hallie frowned at the individual piles of boots, fire hats, and clothing.

"That's intentional. Seconds can mean the difference between life and death, and between preserving or losing a structure. To deploy quickly, we lay our hats and protective gear near our vehicles. Our clothing is heat- and fire-resistant, and the boots are steel-toed to protect our feet from falling debris. Seventy pounds of added weight. There's Miranda."

With a smile, the secretary exchanged the too-big observer vest for a smaller one. Waving good-bye, she climbed the stairs to the main floor and front desk.

"I laid out my stuff when I first arrived this morning," Owen continued, pointing out his things. "Why don't you set that vest next to my boots?"

Hallie did, then snapped a photo. "If a fire call comes in, you and the rest of the crew put your protective clothing on and I slip into my vest. What should I do then?"

"Hop into the engine with us, buckle up and ride along. I assume you read the ride-along rules, but we should review them anyway. Your role is to observe but not participate. No questions during a call—we have things to do and don't need the distraction. No handling equipment, either. During an emergency event, you're free to shadow me as long as you don't interfere. In the case of an actual fire, you're to remain out of harm's way, in a safe area away from the incident."

Hallie nodded. "Got it. May I take photos at a fire?"

"I don't see why not. You'll need the captain's okay to use them in your article."

"Of course. What do you do between calls?"

"Look around and you'll see there's plenty to keep us busy. After an event we make sure the garage and equipment are clean and everything is in good working order for the next call. That includes restocking supplies in each vehicle. We also write up incident reports and work on any assignments from the captain.

"This afternoon I'll put together materials for tomorrow's teacher safety training and make sure my PowerPoint presentation is working."

"If you need any help..."

"I will."

Knowing she could be useful made shadowing Owen even more interesting. Most of the crew had finished their tasks and left the area, but Owen seemed unhurried.

"What else do you do during down time?" Hallie asked.

"Take refresher courses and do quite a bit of in-house training to keep ourselves up to date. This is physically demanding work and we need to stay in shape. There's a gym on the second floor we use whenever possible."

She pictured a dozen buff crew members lifting weights and exercising, and mentally fanned herself. Talk about a great photo op for her article.

Owen gave her a funny look. "What are you smiling at?"

"Nothing. Do you ever relax?"

"Sure. When possible, we take a coffee break. Sometimes we play cards or board games. Come on, I'll show you where that pole ends."

He led Hallie to a small alcove on one side of the apparatus bay she hadn't noticed. She peered upward, to the top of the passageway, and swallowed. "Seems like a long way between the second floor and here."

"Piece of cake—if you do it correctly. Using the pole instead of the stairs shaves valuable seconds off a quick exit. Let's head for the second floor and I'll demonstrate how it's done."

~

"Not all fire departments have these things," Owen told Hallie as they neared the gleaming pole on the second floor. "We consider ourselves lucky."

She nodded, then scribbled something in her notebook. He liked that she paid attention.

"Sliding down the pole correctly takes strength and agility," he said. "We look for a controlled descent and a safe landing on both feet."

"Safe landing?"

"I've seen guys tear their Achilles tendon or roll an ankle. Before my time, some kid on a school field trip tried to shinny up this thing. He got just far enough up that when he fell, he broke his leg."

"That's awful!"

"Yep, and it's why we don't allow kids near the pole without supervision. I'll demonstrate the correct way to slide down."

He removed his shoes and stepped into position in his socks. "I use the arches of my feet to center myself on the pole. My hands keep me there. Watch and learn."

Gripping the pole, he held himself in place while he demonstrated. "Arch one foot against the pole, grasp with both hands, then arch the other foot to the pole." Aside from bulging biceps, he didn't seem the least bit taxed from the effort. "And down I go."

Moments later he landed on the lower level.

"That was awesome!" Hallie called down to him.

Her enthusiasm matched that of the kids he'd shown around, and he couldn't stop his amused grin. "I'll be right up."

Not long after he rejoined Hallie, she eyed the pole, shifted her weight and smoothed her hair. "I'm not a fan of heights, but I'd like to try this."

No adult visitor had ever asked. Owen hesitated. "I don't know. I wouldn't want you to hurt yourself."

"If you train me like you would a recruit...

Knowing how using the pole feels will help me write about it. What do you say?"

Between her wide, pleading eyes and her bottom lip clasped hopefully between her teeth, denying her was impossible. "All right—if you pass the safety lesson."

"Thank you." She toed out of her sneakers and stepped toward the pole.

Owen talked her through the technique and the safety tips. She followed his instructions to the letter. Confident she understood exactly what to do, he nodded. "Let's give this a try. One foot on the pole, then grasp with both hands."

Hallie nodded, sucked in a breath, and followed his instructions. Arms shaking with effort, she settled the other foot in place.

"Hold that pose." He dashed down the stairs, entered the apparatus bay and strode to the base of the pole. "How are you doing?"

"My arms are killing me, but using my feet helps."

"You're ready. Loosen your grip a fraction and come down."

To his relief, she executed the slide perfectly. "Great job," he said after she landed safely. "You're a natural."

"I am, aren't I? It wasn't scary at all." She beamed with pride. "You're a good teacher. "

Some of her hair had worked loose and hung in wisps on either side of her flushed face. Owen brushed the strands behind her ears. "That's been bothering me."

Catching a whiff of her lilac scent, he sniffed appreciatively. "You smell nice."

"Thanks."

Her eyelids lowered a fraction and her head tilted up in a silent but unmistakable invitation for a kiss. Eager to oblige, he stepped closer and cupped her nape.

Just then Hank and Max entered the apparatus bay, their voices growing louder as they drew nearer. Owen and Hallie jerked apart.

"Pole lesson," he explained.

Max raised his eyebrows. "Never seen a lesson like that."

Hank started to add something, but Owen cut in. "Shut it."

Her face beet red, Hallie glanced around. "Where's the ladies' restroom?"

"Main floor, out the security door, to your right," Owen said.

She almost ran up the stairs.

As she disappeared from view, Hank shook his head. "Putting the moves on her when she's shadowing you for a magazine article... Not smart."

Owen agreed. "I sure as hell didn't plan it. Nothing happened, I swear."

But damn, he'd almost kissed her—right here at the station, where anyone could walk in. Hank and Max had.

Talk about improper behavior. He could get in a load of trouble, was dumbstruck that he'd forgotten himself. Blame it on the inviting woman and her slightly parted lips.

Screw that excuse. He owed her an apology.

He wouldn't touch her again while she shadowed him, but he sure wouldn't mind getting to know her later. Trouble was, she didn't strike him as a woman interested in sex and nothing else. Still licking the wounds Colleen had inflicted, he couldn't handle anything more.

Hallie Sawyer was off-limits.

After a quick stop at the top to put on her shoes and grab her phone and camera, Hallie headed for the main floor and the station's ladies' room. She splashed water on her flushed cheeks and gave herself a mental thrashing. She was here to gather information, period, from the expert. Yet the instant Owen had tucked her hair behind her ears, her reasons for shadowing him had faded away.

Aching for his kiss, she'd wanted only to step into the warmth of his arms. The truth was, she'd wanted that since this morning. This strong attraction to Owen must be left over from her high-school crush days. Ridiculous, really, when she hadn't thought of him in years.

"No more crush," she firmly declared out loud, burying any feelings for him deep inside where they wouldn't bubble up again.

As she repaired her makeup, the intercom squawked to life with the announcement of a fire. Her heart in her throat, Hallie made a hasty exit from the bathroom, signaled for Miranda to let her back through the security door, and hurried down the stairs.

~

BEFORE DISPATCHER SARAH MCCONE'S voice finished crackling over the intercom, Owen had donned his firefighting gear. He didn't have time to wait for Hallie and hoped she knew to return to the apparatus garage pronto.

Seconds after the rest of the crew arrived and suited up, she arrived and slipped into her vest.

"Into the truck, stat," he ordered, his need for haste making him terse. "Get in the back and buckle up."

Without a word, she quickly obeyed. Owen followed, along with Hank, Adam, and Gus. Liam, who was licensed to drive the engine, climbed into his seat and slammed the door.

"Where to?" he asked as he pushed the button that raised the enormous garage door.

Riding shotgun, Adam tapped the computer between the seats and read the address out loud. As the yawning garage door opened fully, Liam started the siren. The engine sped through the door and turned onto the street.

Behind them, a wailing aid car followed.

"Twenty-nine seconds," Gus commented. "Not bad."

"Apartment building, fourth floor," Adam read from the screen.

The department didn't own an engine with an attached ladder. While Adam continued to read off information and directed Liam to the site of the fire, Owen, Hank, and Gus discussed which portable ladder to use and otherwise planned as best they could.

Hallie remained quiet—so quiet, she might not have been there at all. Owen glanced over his shoulder at her. Eyes wide with excitement, she watched and listened and no doubt brimmed with questions he had no time to answer.

To his relief, she asked no questions and made no comments. She'd paid attention earlier. He made a mental note to thank her for that, then returned to the matters at hand.

They pulled up to the apartment building. Smoke billowed from the window of the middle units on the fourth floor.

"Stand back, where you see that crowd," he directed her, jerking his chin toward the onlookers.

She nodded. Assured she'd be safe, he pulled on his SCBA breathing apparatus, then grabbed one end of the ladder. Gus took the other end and they pounded toward the building.

6

Hallie and dozens of other onlookers stood some fifty yards back from the building with the apartment, all with eyes on Owen and Gus as they scrambled up the ladder with the hose.

What a great photo for the magazine article. She trained her camera on the scene, but her gaze homed in on Owen. Taking the lead and sure-footed, almost graceful, he moved upward at lightning speed, as if his heavy fireproof clothing, SCBA breathing apparatus, and the bulky hose weighed nothing. Impressed and filled with respect she snapped dozens of photos, both of him alone and with Gus.

At street level, Hank attended the open fire hydrant, while Liam and Adam strode rapidly through the front door.

The window of the burning apartment gaped open, and acrid smoke billowed out. Hallie sent up a silent prayer that Owen, his crewmates, and anyone inside the building stayed safe.

Within seconds the two big men reached the top of the ladder and climbed through the narrow window, as agile as mountain lions.

Hallie soon learned that most of her gawking companions lived in the building. "What happened?" she asked a silver-haired man.

Shoving his hands into his Bermuda shorts pockets and staring down at the white socks pulled almost to his knees, he shook his head. "The wife and I live on the fifth floor just above that apartment. We were at the kitchen table, reading the paper, when we smelled smoke. We barely had time to comment on it before the fire alarm went off."

His wife nodded, chafing her arms as if cold—despite the sweltering day. "I grabbed my purse, Bud got his wallet, and here we are."

The smoke had stopped pouring out the window. A blink on an eye later, a coughing, a white-haired woman exited the front door, escorted by Adam. He guided her to the aid car, where Tony, Nate and Ethan, this month's paramedics, stood ready.

Distraught, the coughing woman attempted to return to the building. "Please, let me go back inside. My cat, Gregory, is up there!"

"You inhaled quite a bit of smoke, ma'am, and our paramedics are waiting to take care of you," Adam said in a matter-of-fact voice meant to calm. "We'll do our best to find Gregory." Wearing a grave expression, he pulled a portable radio from his pocket and spoke into it as he returned to the building.

While the paramedics examined the woman, she spoke loudly as if hard of hearing. "Gregory has been with me since he was a kitten and I rescued him from the dumpster. I can't lose him—he's all I have."

Her voice broke, and Hallie's heart went out to her.

"If anyone can save your cat, our firefighters will," Nate replied comfortingly.

On the heels of his comment, Owen appeared in

the window, his face all but obscured by the SCBA. In one big hand he held a large tabby cat. With his free hand, he gave a thumbs-up.

Aww. Hallie let out a heartfelt sigh.

"Look, Loretta!" someone shouted. "That firefighter has your Gregory."

"Thank the Lord." Loretta sank onto a chair one of the men had set up for her.

The entire group whooped and cheered. Owen nodded before disappearing inside.

In what seemed like no time he tromped through the door with Gregory. He pulled off the SCBA and brought the tom to Loretta, who wept openly. "Thank you so much for saving my baby."

Owen accepted her gratitude with a nod and modest shrug.

He must have sensed Hallie's gaze. His eyes warm, he tipped his firefighter hat her way. The feelings she'd stuffed inside burst free, along with something deeper she didn't want to think about.

"Is that man your boyfriend?" a woman about her age asked.

Hallie shook her head and gestured at her orange vest. "I'm writing a magazine article about the Guff's Lake Fire Department. I'm following him around to chronicle a day in the life of a firefighter."

"I'll follow him anywhere," the woman murmured. "Him and his friends."

Who could argue with that?

Hunkered down in front of Loretta, he patted the cat. "Gregory seems to be in good shape. No smoke damage that I can detect, but you may want your vet to check him out."

With a look of pure relief, she nodded. "I will. I feel

all right, but the paramedics say I should visit the ER and get myself checked. What do you think?"

"I'd trust them with my life, ma'am. You should do what they say."

Loretta gave a reluctant nod and then bit her lip. "Did the fire do much damage?"

"Your living room is in rough shape, and the whole apartment reeks of smoke. How did this happen?"

Loretta combed her hair with her shaky fingers. "I dropped a cigarette in the trash. Guess I should have stubbed it out better. Maybe it's time I quit smoking." She turned to the couple who lived above her. "Will you call the vet and take care of Gregory while I'm gone?"

They nodded. Moments later, the paramedics trundled Loretta into the aid car and headed for the ER.

After Liam and Adam inspected the rest of the building and declared it safe, the crowd disbursed. Owen nodded to Hallie. "As soon as we finish cleanup we'll head back."

HAVING WORKED through the noon hour, Owen, his crewmates and Hallie had missed lunch. By the time they reached the station, the adrenaline rush that accompanied every emergency had worn off and they were all hungry. First, though, they needed to change, clean the engine and prep for the next call. Hallie stood back and took photos.

When the job was done they tromped upstairs.

After washing up, they sat down at the table with their food. Ravenous, Owen dug in. "What did you think about the ride-along?" he asked Hallie when his empty belly began to fill.

"Very exciting." Hallie shook her head. "You were amazing."

The admiration in her eyes made Owen uncomfortable. He shifted in his chair. "Just doing my job."

"It's quite a job. You're a real hero—all of you." Her gaze included Adam, Gus, Hank, and Liam, who looked every bit as awkward from the praise.

"We appreciate that you kept nice and quiet on the way to and from the call," Owen said.

He locked eyes with her until she shifted her focus to stuffing the remains of her meal into her lunch bag.

Adam pushed to his feet. "Gotta do some paperwork." He nodded at Gus, Hank, and Liam. "Coming with?"

The three men filed out with Adam, leaving Owen and Hallie alone.

"Now is a good time for questions," he said. "If you have any."

"Any? I have bunches." After opening her notebook she poised her pen.

She wasn't kidding about the questions. Owen spent a good while answering about a dozen of them.

"This is great info," she said when he finished. "What's next on the agenda?"

"Getting the handouts and the PowerPoint presentation ready for tomorrow's workshop. We'll do that in the big training room, where we met with the captain last week."

There they photocopied and collated materials into packets to hand out, chatting while they worked.

"This looks like an interesting session," she commented, wearing the eager expression he'd begun to anticipate. "I'm sure I'll learn a lot."

"Let's hope everyone else will, too. You know, the other day I found you in my sister's yearbook," he said. "You look completely different now."

"I should hope so." She laughed. "I was pretty homely."

"Nah, you were cute. But I like you better now." He didn't hide his appreciative gaze.

Seeming ill at ease, she began straightening the packets into neat piles. This seemed a good time to apologize for earlier.

Owen cleared his throat. "About what happened after your pole lesson... I was out of line."

"I haven't even thought about that," she said with a dismissive wave of her hand. The sudden flush staining her cheeks told him otherwise. "Bangs in my eyes drive me nuts, too, only sometimes I get so involved in what I'm doing I forget all about them."

He'd seen evidence of that numerous times today. Her interest and excitement about firefighting turned him on. He wanted to kiss her, see if she tasted as good as she looked. Instead he shoved his hands in his pockets. "So we're okay?"

He had no idea why he asked or why her reply mattered so much when he wasn't planning to see her after tomorrow.

"Absolutely."

Owen released the breath he'd been holding. "Let's box this stuff up."

"Then could we take a break?" she asked.

"We've been in here a couple hours. I don't see why not."

Although working alongside Hallie made what was usually a tedious job fun. Owen liked what he knew of her so far, but he meant to keep his distance.

"You're about to find out one of my favorite ways to relax."

"Playing a board game or cards?"

"Nope. We're going to walk around the block. "

And more questions. "Are you allowed to do that? What if you get another call?"

"We'll stick close to the building so that if need be, I can reach the apparatus bay quickly. I'll notify Adam and we'll go."

"Why Adam?"

"He's our shift lieutenant, the next highest-ranking officer under the captain."

"Good to know. While you talk to Adam, I'll take a few photos of the department from across the street."

He nodded. "Meet you outside in five."

7

In the hours since the fire the temperature had grown oppressive. Stepping outside to meet Owen for a walk felt like entering an oven, and the orange vest didn't help. Hallie crossed to the shaded side of the street to take wide-angle photos of the fire department.

She was framing a shot when Owen shouldered the front door open. In Oakley sunglasses, he could have passed as a celebrity heartthrob. Her wayward heart certainly sighed.

I'm only interested in him as a firefighter, she reminded herself as she snapped his photo.

Liar.

Over the day her attraction to him had only increased.

He strode toward her with a fluid grace, his long legs eating up the distance between them and his lips thinned in what Hallie interpreted as disapproval.

"Is something wrong?" she asked as soon as he reached her.

"I don't want my picture in your magazine article. The calendar photo is bad enough, but at least the money we raised is for a good cause."

"Then I won't use anything I just took of you. I would like to use some action photos from the fire."

"Show them to me."

She pulled up those pictures. Owen bent his head toward the screen, standing so close she felt the heat from his body. His spicy aftershave mingled with the faint odor of sweat and man, a heady combination that further weakened her resolve to keep things on a professional level. Hallie handed him the camera and moved aside.

Clearly oblivious of the chaos he'd created inside her, he fast-forwarded through the images. "These are awesome."

"Thanks." She returned to his side. "What about these? Would you object if I use some of the ones you're in?"

"As long as there are other crew members besides me pictured, I'm good. But check with the captain. Let's cross back over and circle around the station."

They waited for the walk light in companionable silence. "Did today meet your expectations?" Owen asked as they started across.

And then some. "The whole day was amazing, way beyond anything I could imagine."

"I aim to please."

Thanks to his dark reflector lenses, she couldn't see his eyes but she sensed his gaze traveling over her. For some reason, she felt a little breathless. Keeping to the sidewalk, they headed around the building, passing baskets of colorful summer flowers, as well as decorative trees and shrubs and several pedestrians.

"How did you go from working for your family's construction company to writing magazine articles?" Owen asked.

After the usual "Sorry for your loss" comments,

most people skirted away from Hallie's past. Certainly no one besides Paige and family members had ever asked about her career switch.

Hesitating, she considered what to say without going into the details of her devastating grief.

"If the question is too personal, feel free to ignore it," Owen said.

"You answered all my questions. Answering yours is the least I can do." She managed a smile. "As you can imagine, after Simon died and I lost the baby, I was a basket case. I never knew when I'd break down. Having my family ready with tissues to blot the tears —even there were none—only made the situation worse.

"I always felt like they expected me to fall apart. They meant well, but I needed them to see me as a survivor. For my own well-being I had to get away from them. That meant moving away from the family compound and leaving Sawyer Construction. I needed something to occupy my time and a way to pay the bills, but I wasn't ready for a forty-hour-a-week job. Freelance writing seemed the perfect alternative. I enjoy what I do, and I doubt I'll ever go back to regular, full-time work."

"I hear ya. Anyone who writes well has my admiration. I never could write worth crap."

"You don't need to—your strengths lie with firefighting."

"True that." He grinned. Seconds later he sobered. "I'm glad you're doing okay."

"You and me both. I wish my parents could see that, but they still treat me with kid gloves."

"Mine are the opposite—too wrapped up in their own lives to pay attention to anyone else."

"That sounds pretty good to me."

"To a point, maybe. Pearl wouldn't say 'No' if they wanted to visit or offered to watch Opal."

Hallie couldn't hide her astonishment. "You mean they don't?"

"The first weekend after the accident they watched Opal, and they sent flowers after Pearl's surgery. Otherwise, nada."

"Where have they been?"

"Right here. They got remarried about a month before the accident, and they're all wrapped up in each other. Plus they're going to Europe soon to celebrate retying the knot. Prepping for the trip takes up a lot of their free time."

Hallie was getting a picture now. "At least they're helping with Pearl's medical bills, right?"

"They don't have the money for that." He glanced at his watch. "This is my night to cook dinner. I need to get started. You may as well take off. Give me the vest and I'll take it inside." As soon as Hallie complied, he went on. "Before I forget, here's my card." He dug into his shirt pocket, then handed it to her. "Knowing you, you're bound to think of more questions after tomorrow. If you need to contact me, shoot me an email. See you here in the morning."

~

MONDAY NIGHT HALLIE sat at her "office" at the kitchen table and transcribed notes from her day into the Guff's Lake Fire Department folder on her laptop. She was typing away when Paige phoned.

When they'd first become grief support group partners some six months after Paige had lost her husband and Hallie had lost Simon and their unborn daughter, they'd been in constant contact, sometimes calling each other a dozen times a day to keep from diving off the deep end of grief. With the passing of time and Paige's recent remarriage, they no longer needed to touch base as often. Once a week sufficed.

"Hey, newlywed," Hallie said, smiling.

Paige giggled, sounding more like a teenage girl than a thirty-nine-year-old woman. "How did it go at the fire department today?"

Wilbur trotted over, shoved his head onto Hallie's lap and gave a big-eyed pet me look. "It was fantastic," she said, giving him the love he wanted. The attention hog nudged her for more and she pushed him away. "I learned tons—and they let me ride the fire engine to a fire."

"I'm jealous—I want to do that. Guess I'll have to live vicariously through you. Tell me more."

"Did you know firefighters spend part of their time educating the public about fire safety? Owen will be doing a workshop for teachers tomorrow and I get to go with him. I'm sure I'll learn even more."

"No doubt. Shadowing him sounds interesting. You must be enjoying that."

Way too much. "He's a good teacher," Hallie hedged. "Smart and patient. I must have asked fifty questions. He answered each one thoroughly and made sure I understood. Here's something else I never knew about the Guff's Lake Fire Department—they have a fireman's pole."

"Get out." Paige sounded as impressed as Hallie.

"I know," Hallie said. "It's supposed to be used only with a fire call, but Owen fudged the rules for me. After he gave me a safety lesson, he let me slide down."

As fun and instructive as the experience had been, the landing had felt way too intimate. Even now she tingled when she thought about the gentle touch of his fingers tucking her bangs behind her ears. His dark, magnetic gaze and the overpowering desire to kiss him...

"You are so lucky," Paige commented.

Hallie wouldn't have used that particular word. Rash, maybe, or a little crazy. She still couldn't quite believe her own reaction—or Owen's. If not for Hank and Max entering the room, that kiss would have happened. Then she'd have been in big trouble.

"That's one weighty sigh," Paige said. Wilbur cocked his head in agreement. "What am I missing?"

Despite the nine-year age difference between Hallie and her friend, shared grief over losing their partners had brought them close. They knew everything about each other and there were no secrets between them.

For that reason and because Hallie knew she could trust Paige to keep whatever she shared confidential, she admitted the truth. "I'm super attracted to him, and he's so easy to talk to. I like him, Paige."

"It's about time you met a man who caught your eye. I'll bet he likes you, too."

Judging by his warm looks Hallie had assumed so. But... "He gave me his card and instructions to email any questions I might have later. Does that sound like a man interested in me?"

"Maybe he has a girlfriend."

"I wouldn't be surprised. Anyway, I set this thing up to gather information for my article, not find a date. Stepping out of my professional role wouldn't be appropriate."

Although she'd wanted to and almost had. Several times. No more of that.

"For two days, anyway. When Milo asked me out

that first time, I was scared to say yes. It felt like a betrayal to Jacob. And you said—"

" 'It's just one date.' I remember. I'm not afraid to start dating again." Well, maybe a little. "I'm not quite ready, either, but I'm getting close."

"I'd say so. In the three-and-a-half years since we've met, I've never heard you talk about a guy like you just did about Owen."

Hallie had to agree. "Enough about me. How's work?" Paige managed a factory that produced jellies and candies using fruit from local orchards.

"Busy as ever." Paige launched into the company's latest marketing campaign for a new product. Then she dropped a bombshell. "Milo and I are trying to get pregnant."

Ignoring a pang of envy, Hallie squealed in excitement. "And you're just now getting around to telling me?"

She'd always dreamed of having children, but losing the baby had changed that. She doubted she'd ever get past the fear that now enveloped her whenever she thought about pregnancy and the possibility of a miscarriage. Her stomach tightened again.

"That's fast," she added. "You've only been married three months."

"Don't forget that I turn forty in January. I don't have the luxury of waiting a few years."

"Keep me posted."

"Believe me, when it happens you'll be the first to know."

Tired after a long day, Hallie yawned. "Today wore me out. I'm going to turn in early."

"Me, too. Milo and I have a date in bed."

Hallie laughed. "You have that date every night."

"Yeah, but this time it's more than just great sex. If all goes well, tonight we'll make our baby."

"I'll cross my fingers."

"And I'll think of you tomorrow. If you get to do anything half as cool as sliding down a pole and riding a fire engine, call me."

8

Owen's empty belly demanded lunch, but the training session was running late. He glanced around the teachers who filled the auditorium of the Guff's Lake Community Center. "Any final questions?"

When no hands were raised, he nodded. "Thanks for your time and remember to put safety first."

A middle-aged administrator stepped to the podium to lead the applause, and then announced a thirty-minute break before the next session.

Men and women stood and began to file through the exit. Owen sought out Hallie. In her orange vest she was easy to spot near the back of the room.

Their eyes met. She gave him a thumbs-up and smiled warmly, as if they were more than acquaintances. His body liked the idea.

Not gonna happen. Knowing that hadn't stopped him from fantasizing about getting physical with her. He'd even started an erotic dream featuring the two of them. A fire alarm had put an end to the fun—right before the good stuff. Just his luck, but probably for the best.

Several teachers approached with comments and

questions about future trainings for their students. Owen directed them to Hank's card in the training packet.

Several women around his age approached him with flirty smiles. He wasn't what you'd call good-looking, but for some crazy reason the ladies had always liked him. The publication of the calendar had only added to whatever it was that drew their attention. He'd grown used to the open flirtations and I'm-interested expressions, even enjoyed it.

One, a blonde in red lipstick, lingered until the others moved away. She tilted her head and smiled seductively. "I'm Erica. Here's my card."

With her short, sassy hair, long legs, and nice body, she was exactly Owen's type. Yet for some reason she didn't do much for him.

Hallie hung back. He gestured her forward, Erica following his gaze. "I see," she said, as if she'd figured something out. She leaned in so that he could look down her V-neck top and lowered her voice. "If that goes wrong, call me. I jotted my cell number on the back of the card."

That as in Hallie and him? If Erica thought they had something going on, she was off by a mile. Owen packed up the laptop he'd brought for his PowerPoint.

"Do you know that woman?" Hallie asked as she joined him.

"Just met her."

"She was flirting with you. I'll bet your girlfriend wouldn't like that."

"I don't have a girlfriend."

"Oh. I'll gather up the extra handouts." Off she went.

She came back empty-handed. "I didn't find any. What else can I do?"

"Not a thing. We're done here."

"That was an informative presentation," she said as they turned toward the exit. "I learned quite a bit."

"Let's hope the teachers did, too."

He caught a whiff of her lilac scent and something uniquely hers underneath. His body went hard and it was all he could do to keep from backing her into the shadows and kissing her.

He needed a woman and soon, someone wanting release and nothing more. That'd cure him of his lust for Hallie.

Erica's card lay heavy in his pocket. Too bad he wasn't interested. After crumpling it up and tossing it in the trash, he shouldered the door open and followed Hallie out.

BEFORE OPENING the passenger door of the Guff's Lake Fire Department sedan Owen had driven to the training, Hallie shrugged out of the orange vest and tossed it into the back. Once she buckled up, Owen headed out of the parking lot.

He hadn't said a word since they'd left the community center. Weariness etched his face, but then his team had handled two fire calls last night. She'd heard a little about them at breakfast, but hadn't had time to learn any details before she and Owen had left for the community center. Nor had the subject come up on the drive over, as most of that conversation had been about the training. She still didn't know anything—except that exhaustion alone couldn't account for the tense set of his jaw.

"Was it something I said?" she said, hoping for a grin.

His lips quirked in a hint of a smile. "I could use an intravenous infusion of caffeine and a sixteen-ounce steak with the works."

"I can't help with either. I'm hungry, too."

"That settles it—we're stopping at Burger Mania."

Her mouth watered, and she was glad she'd brought her purse with her. "I haven't eaten there in ages. But shouldn't you get back?"

"Not just yet. One of the perks of teaching a class midday is taking extra time for lunch."

Minutes later Owen pulled into the drive-up lane, behind several cars.

"Tell me about last night's fires," Hallie said as the car inched forward.

"The first call came in around ten-thirty. A sixteen-year-old boy dumped smoldering coal cinders from a barbecue grill into the trash bin. The trash caught fire and produced a lot of smoke, but no one was hurt."

"Thank goodness."

Owen nodded. "Then around two a.m. a drunk driver crashed his car into a shed. The car caught fire and so did the shed. The driver went to the hospital. He's bruised up, but otherwise okay. His car and the shed are toast. He got a ticket for DUI."

"Sounds like he deserved it. Did you get any sleep?"

"Couple hours."

Hallie shook her head. "No wonder you need caffeine."

"Always when I'm on the job, but making do with limited sleep is a given. We're almost at the order box. What do you want?"

"A cheeseburger and a lemonade."

"Is that enough?"

"It's plenty."

Owen placed her order plus two large cheeseburgers with the works, black coffee and a jumbo order of fries for himself.

Hallie dug a ten-dollar bill from her purse and tried to give to him, but he refused to take it. "This is on me."

With money tight she wasn't about to argue. Once they were at the pick-up window he handed her the food bags and set the drinks in cup holders.

Everything smelled delicious. Instead of pulling over to eat on the premises, he drove toward the exit.

Hallie frowned. "We're taking this back to the station?"

"Heck, no."

"Then where are we going?"

"You'll see."

A few miles up the road he signaled and turned into a wooded area. To Hallie's surprise, a deserted parking area greeted them, and beyond it, an airy space that felt private and secluded.

"This is pretty," she said, looking around. "You'd never guess Kirkdale Road is mere yards away. What is this place?"

"It's called Truver Park. It's a pocket park—a tiny park in an unlikely location."

"You're telling me." She glanced around. "I see picnic tables over there."

"That's where we're headed." Owen grabbed a packet of moist wipes from the glove compartment and handed it to Hallie. "You're in charge of these."

"I've lived in Guff's Lake all my life, but never knew this existed," she said as they strolled toward a table under a lofty oak.

"My grandparents live nearby. When Pearl and I were kids and things got rough at home, we'd stay with them, walk over here, and hang out."

Hallie hadn't realized he'd grown up like that. "The parents who recently remarried."

"One and the same. They fought a lot, especially in the months before they divorced. Which they did twice before I was twelve. The first six to nine months after they remarried were okay. Then things headed south and everything went to hell."

Having grown up in a loving family, she couldn't imagine living with so much turmoil. "Maybe this third time is the charm."

"I wouldn't make any bets. Let's eat."

They sat down at a weathered wood table. Despite the heat, the shade and a light breeze made for a reasonably comfortable picnic spot.

Owen set the fries between them to share. "So you know Samantha Everett."

Hallie nodded. "We were in the same knitting class. That was around the time she and Adam got together. Do you know her well?"

"I've been to their house a couple times. She's great and her bakery stuff is killer. The scones, the muffins. And those cinnamon rolls." He licked his lips and Hallie laughed.

Not counting family, she hadn't felt this comfortable around a man in ages. She could easily grow to like Owen more than was smart. Too bad he wasn't interested.

She bit into her burger. "This is really good."

For a while they were both too busy eating to speak. "Until yesterday, I had no idea firefighters conducted workshops," she said later. "How much training are you required to do?"

"For the public, a couple hours a month, depending. In-house, all the time."

"That sounds fun."

"Never thought of it that way. You fascinate me." He shut his mouth as if he hadn't meant to blurt the words.

No one else had ever described her as fascinating. "Me?"

"You're like a breath of fresh air—excited about learning new things and not afraid to ask questions."

"I do ask my share."

"Times three." He chuckled.

The meal ended. As Hallie stuffed the debris into the empty food bag, ketchup from an open packet dribbled down the front of her white blouse.

"Darn it," she muttered, dabbing the mess with a napkin. The blotch spread. "I need to put cold water on this before it stains. Is there a bathroom around here?"

Owen shook his head.

"Shoot—this is one of my favorite summer blouses."

"Will a moist wipe work?"

"It's worth a try." After a moment of vigorous scrubbing, she sighed. "I got some of the ketchup out, but it's going to leave a stain."

"Let me have a go." Owen swept the trash aside, then patted the picnic table. "Sit."

He opened a fresh wipe and lifted her blouse away from her stomach. "Hold this steady," he said.

Grasping her hem, Hallie held the blouse away from her skin while Owen worked at the red splotch.

She was warm to begin with. Heat from Owen's hands upped her internal temperature to scorching.

"It's fading," he commented, his head bent to the task.

Directly over her lap.

A certain part of got all excited. Pull yourself together—he's only trying to help, she silently chastised herself.

She glanced at the blue sky and the leafy trees. Studied the top of his head. His hair was super short, but she could tell it was nice and straight.

Once or twice his hands bumped her stomach, which only added to the pandemonium inside her. She couldn't think of anything less romantic, yet here she was, desperate to tug his head up and kiss him.

So much for pulling herself together. Hallie frowned. "You have a bit of a cowlick."

"One good reason besides the job to keep my hair short. There—the red is gone."

He straightened, added the used wipes to the rest of the trash, and dried his hands on his thighs. "Once your shirt dries, you'll be good as new."

His gaze flickered to her breasts. She glanced down at the wet spot that stretched from the hem of her blouse to just below her bra.

Worried, she fanned the fabric. "I can't go into the station like this. I'm a mess."

"It's not so bad."

"You can see my stomach through the wet fabric!"

He flashed a cocky grin. "It's a nice stomach."

"Owen! This isn't funny."

Sobering, he sat next to her on the picnic table and checked his watch. "We don't have to head back just yet. The humidity is so low, your blouse should dry fast. But if you're still damp when we get back to the station, call it a day." He shook his head. "Those bangs of yours are in your eyes again."

He smoothed her hair behind her ears, just as he had the day before. This time he lingered, tracing the shells of her ears. All the nerve endings in her body jumped to life. Desire flooded her, too potent to fight.

Hallie forgot everything but Owen and the overwhelming longing to be in his arms.

"We shouldn't do this," he said in a husky voice. "You don't know me."

Whatever that meant.

He started to drop his hands. Placing her hands over his, she stopped him. "It's okay, Owen. I want you to kiss me."

"You sure?"

His heavy-lidded eyes darkened and she could barely think, let alone speak. She swiveled her head and brushed her lips over the inside of his wrist. With a groan, he kissed her.

At last.

9

Hallie's sweet body pressed nice and close. She felt good, even better than Owen had imagined. He touched his tongue to the seam of her lips. Without hesitation they parted and invited him into the wet warmth of her mouth.

Images of her under him, naked and panting, filled his mind. He wanted to ease her down and—

Overhead a crow cawed. That and the soft splat inches from where he sat jerked him back into the here and now.

What in hell was he doing?

With a muffled oath he pulled away. Hallie's eyelids fluttered open. Her dazed expression, flushed skin, and kiss-swollen lips made him think twice about letting her go.

The inappropriateness of the situation—this was a work day, not a date—doused the fire in his belly. He was supposed to show her how he spent his day, not make out with her.

Determined to get on track again, he stood. "It's a good thing that crow had a lousy aim."

"Yuck." Hallie, too, scooted off the table. A slight

frown on her face, she glanced at her shirt and smoothed her fingers over it.

"That shouldn't have happened," he said by way of an apology.

"I didn't exactly stop you." She averted her gaze, making for an awkward moment.

"Hallie." Lifting her chin with his finger, he forced her to meet his eyes. "We kissed a few times and it was nice, that's all."

She nodded. "I have a confession to make. You're the first man I've kissed in four years."

"That's a long time." Since her fiancé's death. Proving she wasn't a casual-sex type woman.

"I know. Can we go back to the station now?"

They deposited the trash in the garbage and made for the car. Owen unlocked the car and then started the engine. The air conditioner spit hot air into the over-heated interior. He grimaced. "It'll cool down soon."

"My blouse is nearly dry. This heat will probably finish the job."

"See, those kisses weren't all bad," he teased. She tensed up. "I'm trying to coax a smile from you."

Her lips barely curled at the corners, and he could only guess what she might be thinking. Time to set her straight so she didn't get the wrong idea. "Listen, I'm a guy with lot of baggage—stuff I rarely talk about that you probably don't want to know. But my story might shed light on where I stand."

"I'd like to hear it."

"I told you about my parents fighting all the time. I swore I'd never be like them. I imagined myself in a marriage similar to what my grandparents have. When I married Colleen, I thought I'd found my for-ever partner." He let out a bitter laugh. "Wrong."

Hallie shot him a curious look. "What happened?"

The car was nice and cool now. Owen paused to adjust the A/C before continuing. "We got married a month before I started college. I wanted kids right away. In high school we'd talked about that and Colleen said she did, too. But between her forty-hour-a-week job and my full load of classes and part-time job, we barely saw each other. We agreed to put off starting a family for a while."

Talking about his ex gave him hives, but he wasn't going to stop now. He checked for traffic and pulled onto Kirkdale Road.

"By my junior year, Colleen had grown tired of being the breadwinner. I've always been good with computers and she suggested I use my skills to bring in extra money. I started a side business designing computer programs and made enough for her to cut back her hours at work. For me it seemed the right time to have a baby, but Colleen was too unhappy."

Looking back, Owen realized he hadn't been happy, either. Somewhere the relationship had taken a wrong turn. He'd tried everything to rekindle the spark between them, refusing to give up even when they were both miserable.

What a fool he'd been.

"A couple weeks before I graduated I got hired at Guff's Lake FD. Between my new salary and my computer business, I made out real well. On a professional level, things were good. In my personal life, not so much. I figured having a kid would help. Colleen decided that it was her turn to earn a college degree. She enrolled in Oregon State University in Beaverton."

Hallie's eyes widened. "That's a long way from here."

"Two hundred-eighty-some miles. I had my dream

job at the station and wasn't about to transfer up there." He stopped at a red light. "For a while we saw each other once or twice a month."

"That must have been difficult for you both."

"You want the truth? We'd been fighting so much it was easier to live apart. As hard-headed as I am I figured we'd work through our problems and come out okay. She had other ideas. The day she graduated she asked for a divorce."

The final blow had been her accusation that he was out of touch with his feelings. Like hell. The pain he'd felt proved otherwise.

"I'm sorry, Owen. "

He shrugged. "I'm over it, and glad I didn't have a kid with her." That would have been a disaster for the child.

"Do you still want children?"

"Yeah, but I don't know that I'll ever have them."

"I hope you get your wish."

She hugged herself as if something hurt. She probably wanted kids, too, but he wasn't going to ask. It wasn't his business.

At least she seemed less tense. This was good. On the downside, sharing his miserable story had dredged up a lot of crap better left buried.

"What I went through is nothing like your situation," he added, shoving his past away. "But it's been tough. I date some, but I'm not looking to get involved in anything serious—now or in the foreseeable future."

"I appreciate knowing that, but don't worry. I'm not even at the dating stage."

Owen blew out a breath and turned into the station parking lot. "It's good to know we understand each other. Rest easy—you're safe with me."

"Easy it is." Hallie flashed a genuine smile that made him feel on top of the world.

"You want to stay awhile longer?"

"I think I'll go home. Thanks for letting me shadow you. My car is just over there, so please let me out here."

He did. "Take care and best of luck with that article. Like I said yesterday, if you come up with more questions, shoot me an email."

"I will."

As she walked away, he stared at her long legs and swaying hips. And knew that for all his talk, he wouldn't forget those red-hot kisses anytime soon.

~

HALLIE WAS HALFWAY home when she realized she'd left her camera in the car Owen had used today. She never left it behind. That just showed how rattled she was about what had happened. Even more unnerving, she'd enjoyed every unforgettable second with him.

The man sure knew his way around a kiss. Her lips still tingled—and so did her most intimate female parts. After four long years, her body had awakened famished.

She half-wished he'd asked her out but she hadn't given him the chance. She smacked her forehead. "Why did I say I wasn't dating?"

Because she wasn't. Since he didn't want to get involved he probably wouldn't have asked anyway. Hallie wasn't ready for anything close to a relationship, either, but—

She cut herself off. No point thinking about it when she doubted she'd see him again.

The dreary thought left her conflicted and confused. She considered calling Paige, but her friend was at work and this wasn't important enough to disrupt her day.

Hallie returned to the problem of her camera. She hated not having it with her. Maybe she should drive back to the station and get it. A glance at the gas gauge changed her mind. Almost on empty. With her bank account in the same dismal condition she couldn't afford to waste the fuel.

Any day now she should receive payments for articles that had been published in various magazines. She expected at least one check in this afternoon's mail, but they didn't always arrive on time.

Having money in the bank again sure would be nice. She could pay the bills and put funds away for emergencies and the travel required if John Bodine, the editor at Fire Prevention magazine, okayed the fire department series.

"If there are any financial gods listening, now would be a good time for me to receive what I'm owed," she said aloud.

Living without a regular income sucked, but the freedom of working when and where she chose more than compensated for the uncertainty.

For now she would have to manage without the camera. No problem, as last night she'd downloaded the photos Captain Comings had approved to her laptop. She would ask Miranda to keep the camera safe for a few days.

When she let herself into the cottage, Wilbur bounded toward her with a happy woof, making her smile despite her worries.

"I'm going to change clothes and call Miranda," she told him. "Then you and I are going for a nice, long walk."

After exchanging her blouse and slacks for shorts and a tank top, Hallie spoke briefly with Miranda. She couldn't help but wonder where Owen was and what he was doing.

Was he thinking about those kisses?

The longing started up all over again. With a sigh, she texted Paige about getting together soon.

Her impatient dog wagged his tail and barked at the leash hanging on the hook near the door.

"All right, all right."

She managed to grab her iPod and tether Wilbur to his leash before he tugged her out the door. Earbuds in place, she tuned to the audio mystery novel she was halfway through—a riveting story guaranteed to help her forget all about Owen Ayers.

10

―――――

After Owen's forty-eight-hour stint at the station ended he headed to Rosemary's Breakfast Nook with Max, Hank, and Liam. The restaurant was packed—it always was—but Rosemary had reserved their usual booth.

Coffeepot in hand and a ready smile, the forty-something restaurant owner bustled over. Owen nodded and slid wearily across the seat.

"Must have been a busy night," she commented, filling the mugs with steaming coffee.

"Second one in a row." Liam rubbed his hand over his shaved head. "Keep the coffee coming."

"You got it. Do you all want your regular orders?" Owen and the others nodded, and Rosemary hurried off.

"Anyone up for a run tomorrow before it gets too hot?" Hank asked.

Max and Liam had plans elsewhere. A hard run appealed to Owen, but he was still struggling with the computer training program. With only two weeks and counting until the promised release date, he couldn't afford the time away. "Not this weekend."

Over the next several days he'd likely pull several

all-nighters. Tonight, though, he intended to sleep like the dead. Not even fantasizing about Hallie would keep him up. Emphasis on up. He hadn't been this crazed about a woman in he didn't know how long.

Max elbowed him. "Earth to Owen. I said, it's been awhile since you had a thing for a woman."

Owen frowned. "What?"

"Hallie," his bud clarified. "It's obvious you like her."

"Your point is?"

"Gonna ask her out?"

Even if he wanted to, and he did, he'd assured her she was safe with him. In other words, no dating. "She's been through a lot, man," he said. "I'm the last guy she needs."

"She could say the same thing about you. Maybe when you drop off her camera you two can lick each other's wounds." Max's smart-ass mouth quirked.

Owen narrowed his eyes in warning and his crewmate held up both hands. "I was only kidding around. You need to get some sleep."

Couldn't argue with that. Owen wasn't sure why he'd stopped at Miranda's desk and announced he would deliver Hallie's camera this morning—within hearing distance of his crewmates—when she didn't seem to need it right away.

Hell, he didn't even want to see her. Not at all. He let out a derisive snort at that load of bull.

Breakfast arrived and they all dug in. He would drop off the camera and leave, he decided while he ate. Then head home and work on the program until he crashed.

"Back to Hallie," Hank commented after Rosemary brought their checks and they paid up. "As attractive as she is, I'd go nuts if she or anyone followed me around all day. You did great. The captain knew what he was going when he assigned the job to you."

The captain and everyone else would think differently if they knew about those kisses. Owen shrugged. "I did what I was told."

"Now she has the info she needs to write a good article," Owen's bud added. "The Guff's Lake FD already rocks, but positive press is never a bad thing. And in a national magazine—that's big."

When Owen's crewmates turned toward the exit he nodded at the bakery counter. "I should pick up cinnamon rolls for Pearl and Opal." And one for Hallie. "See you Monday."

Moments later, bakery sack in hand, Owen strapped himself into the Jag and headed for her place.

~

SEATED at the kitchen table Hallie lifted her hair off her neck, pulled it into a ponytail and secured it with a hair band. Geez, it was hot—almost too hot to think about working on the article.

At not quite ten in the morning the cottage's aging air conditioner fought a losing battle to cool the place down. Insulation and double-pane windows would make a world of difference, but the landlord had no interest in upgrading the rental house. Even Wilbur seemed listless. He'd plopped down in front of the kitchen air vent and hadn't stirred since.

Hallie got up, moved to the sink, and splashed cold water on her face. She wandered back to the table and her mountain of notes. So much information to organize.

She started with the photos she'd downloaded.

Keeping in mind that Owen didn't want certain pictures of him in the article, she selected several he'd approved from the fire at the apartment building and a group photo from the meeting Monday morning.

Such big, handsome, heroic guys. Owen was by far the most attractive. The dreamy sigh that slipped out drew Wilbur's attention.

"It's nothing," she assured him. And silently ordered herself not to think about Owen—for about the umpteenth time since yesterday. Shadowing him for two days had served its purpose. He wasn't going to ask her out and she needed to forget him and move on.

Fat chance. Lying in bed in her overheated room last night, she'd revisited the feel of his solid chest against her breasts, his eager mouth on hers... Hot and restless and aching with feelings those kisses had unlocked, she'd lain awake for hours.

Her female parts got all turned on again. She crossed her legs and gave up working. Moments later she filled a glass with cold lemonade from the refrigerator. While she drank it, she looked out the window above the sink.

The grass in the front yard, watered sparingly after dark last night, looked thirsty and sad. Even the woods on either side of the house and across the dirt road drooped. "I can't work here," she muttered at Wilbur. "We need to go someplace where I can concentrate."

Wilbur eyed her as if he were saying Show me the money, before settling back into nap-land.

"Have you forgotten the two checks that came in yesterday's mail?" she reminded him. Enough money to pay bills and put some away. "You went with me to make a deposit at the ATM and fill the tank with gas. We can go anywhere."

The question was, where?

A cool café where she could sip an ice coffee and work in relative comfort sounded good. But Hallie hadn't bothered to straighten her hair today—too hot—and she didn't want to be seen with her hair this out of control. Besides, she didn't know of a café that allowed animals inside. The dog park on the south side of town had a doggie swimming hole. That might be fun, at least for Wilbur. Although she wouldn't be able to work there. And she needed to—

A low-slung convertible pulled up the gravel drive and braked to a stop beside the carport.

She'd never seen a bronze car before. The rich color and sleek lines alone made for a sexy combo. The man behind wheel catapulted the sight into breath-catching territory.

Owen.

So much for forgetting about him.

In a blue T-shirt, faded jeans, sandals, and his Oakleys, he strode across the yard, his long-legged stride powerful and graceful. Hallie's wayward heart lifted and her body hummed before she caught herself.

They'd said their good-byes yesterday. She certainly hadn't expected to see him again. What was he doing here?

Curious and a little nervous—though she couldn't have said why—she turned away from the window. Moments before Owen knocked on the door, Wilbur jumped up and barked sharply.

"Hush." She headed for the front of the cottage, wishing she'd straightened her hair after all and dressed in something other than raggedy cutoffs and a tank top. After tightening the band around her ponytail—for all the good that'd do—she pasted a polite expression on her face and opened the door. "Hello, Owen."

"Hi." His gaze flitted from her head to her breasts, down her legs, and flip-flops before he jerked his eyes up to her face.

Now she felt even hotter, but she wasn't about to let on. Or ask him in, which seemed dangerous. She slipped outside, bringing Wilbur with her, and shut the door behind her.

Owen held her camera case in one big hand. "Thought you might need this and a cinnamon roll from Rosemary's," he said in a gruff voice.

He'd brought the camera and a treat? She almost melted. "How did you know I've been craving a cinnamon roll? Meet Wilbur."

Pleased to have company, the lab yipped happily and wagged his tail.

Owen's guarded expression faded. "Hiya, big guy." He hunkered down and rubbed between Wilbur's ears.

In doggie heaven, Wilbur almost moaned with joy. When the patting stopped, he sat down and raised his paw.

"He wants to shake your hand," Hallie said.

Grasping the offered paw, Owen obliged. "You're a smart one, Wilbur."

"Pretty wily, too—as the patched-up holes under the fence and the dug-up flower beds there can attest."

The big goofball cocked his head and whined. "Don't play contrite with me," Hallie said, but she couldn't help smiling.

Birds twittered and in the distance a dog barked. He returned a friendly woof.

"I haven't been out here in the country in years,"

Owen said. "It's pretty and a good ten degrees cooler than downtown."

"But still miserably hot."

He'd come all the way out here to deliver her camera and the treat. What could she do but invite him in? "Would you like a cold drink?"

After hesitating he shrugged. "Sure."

As Hallie led him through the door, she knew he was looking at her bare legs.

He glanced around the living room. "Cozy."

"You mean small, but the big yard and the privacy more than make up for the lack of space. I'm comfortable here."

"Do you own it?"

"If I did I'd fix it up. The rent is cheap, though, and the landlord gave me the okay to paint it. It took me six months to finish both the inside and outside. I think I did a decent job."

"No one helped you?"

"My family offered, but I wanted to do it myself."

She led him into the cramped kitchen. Funny, it felt even tinier now. "I have lemonade or coffee left over from breakfast. I can add ice. Are we going to share the cinnamon roll?"

"Nope—I had mine at breakfast. This one is all yours. Iced coffee sounds good." He nodded at the laptop on the table. "You're working."

"Organizing my notes and photos from the station and mulling over the best way to approach the article."

Hallie wanted to bring it all to life in a way that pleased John Bodine and brought in positive feedback from magazine subscribers. In case he needed an extra nudge to okay the series.

"You're a smart, experienced writer—you'll figure it out."

Owen thought she was smart? Glowing, she moved the laptop to the counter to make room at the two-person table. "Please, sit down."

He took a seat. Hallie filled a pitcher with ice and cold coffee. She set it and two glasses on the table, along with the bag containing the cinnamon roll.

Unable to resist, she dug it from the bag as soon as she sat down. She took a bite. "Oh, this is good," and went back for more. Soon the whole thing was gone.

Owen grinned. "I've never seen so much enthusiasm for a cinnamon roll."

"Hey, it was made by Samantha." Not wanting to waste a single crumb, she used her finger to collect crumbs from the tabletop.

His hooded eyes followed her finger into her mouth and she forgot all about the crumbs.

He shifted in his chair and his knees bumped hers, throwing her insides into chaos.

Hallie scooted back a fraction and held her icy glass to the skin above her breasts bared by her tank top. Owen's expression heated, adding to the fire flaring inside her. If he made a pass at her she wasn't going to stop him.

Really, Hallie? Shouldn't she get to know him better first? It seemed the smart thing to do.

Determined to behave herself, she set the glass down. "That's some car you drive. It's a Jaguar, right?"

He nodded. "A limited edition XK8. My present to myself after the divorce."

He sat back and half-drained his coffee, his throat working. Even that turned her on. Man, was she in trouble.

"Did you get any sleep last night?" she asked, sweetening her coffee with milk and sugar.

"Maybe four hours."

"That's two nights in a row. I don't know how you can even sit up straight."

"I'm used to it. I'll catch up tonight."

He rolled his broad shoulders and stretched, his T-shirt straining to accommodate his powerful torso. Oh, dear God, couldn't he cut her a break?

He toyed with a smile. "Careful, or you'll stir that coffee to death."

Hallie removed the spoon.

Silence stretched between them, fraught with things unsaid and feelings she fought to contain. She made a show of brushing any remaining crumbs from the table.

Owen cleared his throat. "Did you think of any more questions for me?"

Last night she'd thought of a few, but at the moment her entire focus centered on resisting the urge to tug him up and kiss him again.

"Not at the moment." Panicky and needing him to leave, she stood. "I should get back to work."

"Yeah, me, too."

"Didn't you just finish your shift?"

"This has nothing to do with firefighting. I kept my secondary career developing computer programs. The current project involves updating a safety training program I created several years ago. It's used by firefighters around the country."

"Wow. Is Captain Comings okay with that?"

"As long as it doesn't interfere with my job or reflect negatively on the department."

"I'm impressed. But if it were me I'd go home and sleep twelve hours."

"I wish, but I set a deadline I need to meet. Sleep will have to wait until tonight." He drained his glass. "Thanks for the coffee."

"Thank you driving all the way out here with my camera and for bringing me some deliciousness." She walked him to the door.

He glanced at her mouth and she longed for a kiss all over again. She busied herself keeping Wilbur from dashing outside.

Owen cleared his throat. "Take care."

"You too."

Hallie closed the door. Sagging against the unyielding wood, she listened as the wheels of the Jaguar crunched over the gravel. She didn't draw in a normal breath until he drove away.

11

"Hey, big brother," Pearl called out when Owen entered the house. "You look beat but you also seem somehow wired."

"Not enough rest and too much coffee."

Plus a hefty dose of lust. Hallie hadn't been easy to resist this morning, and the short cutoffs and a snug tank top didn't help.

"Where's Opal?" he asked, his desire making him sound gruff to his own ears.

Pearl lifted her eyebrows. "She's in her room, getting ready for a birthday party. We'll be gone several hours, enough time for you to nap off your bad mood."

Owen ignored the crack. "I can't afford it today—I need to be in my office, working. At least one of us is rested."

"I slept better than I have in ages and feel great. My back hardly bothered me last night."

"That's good news."

"Especially with work starting next week. I've been thinking that before I go back I should get together with Hallie. If it's okay with you, I'll invite her over here Friday night. That way you can see her, too—

since she shadowed you around and you're friends now." Pearl gave a sly smile.

She thought he needed a girlfriend. No, thanks, and Owen didn't want her getting any ideas about Hallie. He had enough of those already. "Can't you meet someplace else?" he asked.

His sister's smile vanished. "You don't want Hallie here."

Oh, he wanted her here. For that matter, everywhere. Under him, calling his name when she climaxed...

"I wouldn't mind meeting her someplace else and would if I had a sitter for Opal," Pearl went on. "Geema and Big Pop are going to dinner with friends, and you have your own life. I can't wait to save enough for my own place. Never mind, I'll get together with Hallie some other time."

Owen hated that long face. "Go ahead and invite her over. If I make enough progress on the training program before Friday night, I'll be at the poker game. And FYI, I don't need your help finding a girlfriend."

"So you keep saying." She glanced at the clock on the microwave. "I'd better hurry Opal up or we'll be late."

"Let me do that," he offered. "I haven't seen her since Sunday night and I probably won't see her any more today."

On the way to his niece's room, he decided to go out Friday night regardless of the progress he made. As hot as he was for Hallie, sticking around here would be way too risky.

~

WHEN WILBUR'S midday frolic at the doggie swimming hole ended, Hallie was dirty and almost as wet as her dog. On the drive home she wrinkled her nose and glanced at him in the rearview mirror. "You stink. But then, so do I. As sweltering as it is, I need to open the window so I can breathe in here."

All tuckered out and secured in his travel harness, Wilbur yawned.

"Bath time for you," she announced when they arrived home.

After tying his leash to a tree, she got out the hose and doggie shampoo. Thanks to the heat he didn't even mind. Clean again, he shook himself off, endured a vigorous toweling and trotted inside.

Hallie marched herself straight to the bathroom, where she enjoyed a refreshing shower. She changed into clean clothes, then brushed her wet hair. At the moment it looked okay, but letting it air dry wouldn't be pretty. It needed to be blow dried and straightened. When she finished, she looked presentable.

She'd broken a sweat again. Ugh. Too antsy to sit at home, she grabbed her laptop. "Time for your nap," she told Wilbur. "I'm going to find a cool place to sit and work. I'll be back later."

Already stretched out in front of the air conditioner with his eyes closed, he didn't appear to care.

Some forty minutes later, seated in a comfortable booth at The Rogue—the Guff's Lake version of Denny's—she nibbled a curly fry from the basket she'd ordered, wiped her hands, and let the words flow onto the screen.

She typed two paragraphs before pausing to dip a fry in ketchup. A gob of the red stuff landed on her tank top, reminding her of the picnic with Owen. He'd worked hard to remove the stain from her blouse with his big, capable hands.

Later, the same hands had tucked her bangs behind her ears, which had led to pressing up nice and close to his gorgeous body and some of the best kisses ever...

Hallie bit back a moan. And wished that this morning she and Owen had continued where they'd left off yesterday.

No, no, no. He'd said nothing about wanting to get to know her, hadn't even hinted at the possibility. Getting physical was out—regardless how badly she wanted to. She wet a napkin in ice water and made quick work of removing all traces of ketchup.

Then she checked her phone and discovered a voice message left while she and Wilbur had splashed around at the doggie park. Having locked her phone in the glove compartment, she hadn't realized. Of all people, the call was from Pearl Ayers.

After listening to the message, Hallie called her back. "Hi, Pearl, this is Hallie. It's so good to hear from you."

They exchanged a few pleasantries before Pearl said, "We need to catch up. Do you want to get together Friday night?"

"I'd love to. Tell me where and what time, and I'll be there."

"Why don't you come to Owen's after dinner?"

Given Hallie's out-of-control feelings, this was not a good idea. "Let's go out instead," she suggested.

"I would if I could, but I don't have a sitter. Besides, I want you to meet Opal. Owen will be at a poker game, so it'll be just us girls."

That sounded safe enough. "Okay."

Pearl gave her the address. They disconnected and Hallie went back to work.

12

___

Hallie was ready to walk out the door Friday night when her sister phoned.

"Chase is working late," Libby announced. "I just put Jimmy to bed and Reese and Bella are outside, playing with their cousins. In other words, we can talk without getting interrupted!"

Hallie laughed. "I wish I could but I'm about to walk out the door."

"Big plans?"

"Pearl Ayers and I are getting together." Hallie didn't add that Pearl lived at Owen's or why. She didn't have time. Besides, Owen wouldn't be there.

"Talk about a blast from the past," Libby said. "You haven't seen her in ages."

"Not since high school."

"Ooh, you can talk about her hunky brother. Which reminds me—did you have fun shadowing him?"

Hallie was tempted to confide in her sister, but she really did have to leave. That and there wasn't all that much to share besides the kisses that weren't going anywhere. "I learned tons. Why don't I call you tomorrow?"

"Okay, but you know how crazy our Saturdays are. Birthday parties, swim lessons, and the usual running around. I may not have time to talk. Love you."

"Mwah." Hallie disconnected. "Gotta go," she told Wilbur. "Be good, hear?"

Reaching Pearl involved a twenty-odd mile drive, but that was true of most everyone Hallie knew. As much as she enjoyed living in the boonies, the distance from her friends did have its drawbacks.

She took Kirkdale Road, which cut straight through town.

Some thirty minutes later, dusk rapidly approaching, Hallie drove over a bridge that crossed the Rogue River. Following the directions from her GPS, she turned into a neighborhood of newer houses and expansive manicured lawns that put her bedraggled yard to shame.

Owen's home sat at the end of a cul-de-sac. Lots of glass and wood, with the living room window reaching two stories high, no doubt to take advantage of the views of the Rogue River and the Siskiyou Mountains on the horizon.

In other words, House Beautiful.

Per Pearl's instructions she pulled up the concrete driveway and stopped beside the two-car garage. Clutching a bottle of wine she headed up a walkway lined with lights. She stepped onto a brick entry and rang the bell.

Pearl greeted her with a warm smile and a hug. "It's so good to see you, Hallie."

"You too. I can't believe we waited all this time to get together. This is for us." Hallie handed her friend the wine.

The little girl standing timidly nearby shared Pearl's round eyes. She wasn't much older than Hallie's daughter would have been if she hadn't miscarried. Despite the ache in her heart, she smiled. "You must be Opal."

Pearl cupped her daughter's shoulders. "This is my friend, Hallie. Say hello and let's invite her in."

Opal waved her fingers. Charmed, Hallie waved back and stepped into an entry as big as her kitchen. "It's nice to meet you, Opal."

"Pink is my favoritist color," Opal announced, apparently over her shyness.

Hallie noted her pink dress and matching sandals. "So I see."

Pearl led her into the living room. Thick rugs, a massive stone fireplace, and masculine furniture made for an impressive room.

"What a beautiful house," Hallie said.

"That's my brother—a man who knows what he wants and makes it happen."

Interesting, and from what Hallie knew about Owen, an apt description.

"I start kindergarten next week," Opal said. "Geema and Big Pop bought me a new dress and shoes!"

"They did? Who are Geema and Big Pop?"

"My grandparents."

"Great-grandparents," Pearl corrected. "Owen coined their nicknames when he was a toddler."

Hallie pictured him as a little boy. Even then his navy eyes must have turned heads.

"Hallie, do you want to see my room?" Opal asked.

"I'd love to."

Pearl nodded. "Then it's time to get ready for bed and go to sleep."

"Okay. It's not really my room," the little girl pointed out as she skipped down the carpeted hallway.

"It is until I save enough for our own place," Pearl said.

"Mama got a new job, and it starts the same day I start kindergarten." Opal scampered into her bedroom.

Wanting to know more, Hallie gave Pearl a questioning look.

"I'll fill you in later," her friend said.

What was obviously a guest bedroom had been transformed into a makeshift child's room, with toys and books and a Disney-themed princess bedspread. Hallie smiled. "Very nice."

She glanced out the window at the back yard and the darkening evening. A small building caught her eye, too big to be a tool shed. "What's in there?"

"That's Uncle Owen's office. He's a firefighter and a computer geek."

Hallie laughed. "You know that word?"

Opal nodded proudly. "It means he likes math and computers. He told me so."

"He's crazy about Opal and vice versa," Pearl said. "Time to get into your nighty, sweetie. Call me when you're ready for bed and I'll come read you a story."

"She's adorable and you are so lucky," Hallie commented as she and Pearl headed back toward the living room.

"Don't I know it. Come with me to the kitchen and we'll open the wine you brought."

The gadget-filled kitchen was every bit as classy as the living room. By the time Pearl opened the wine and filled two glasses, Opal was ready for bed. "I'll be back," Pearl said. "Make yourself at home."

Carrying both glasses, Hallie returned to the living room. Pearl's drink went on an inlaid wood coffee table. Hallie took hers to the oversize leather chair and settled in. The seat cushions were nice and firm, but the leather was soft as a baby's bottom. Owen had excellent taste.

"She's all tucked in. Let me at the wine." Pearl sat down on the couch and slid a throw pillow behind her.

"How's your back?" Hallie asked.

"Getting better by the day, but evenings are a little rough. At the moment I'm okay, but I may stretch out later." She retrieved her glass and lifted it. "To renewing our friendship."

Hallie saluted with hers.

"I love the taste of this," Pearl said, licking her lips. "Can I tell you about Opal?"

"Please do."

"She's the best thing that ever happened to me, and the only reason I'm glad I married Teddy Majors."

"I don't believe I know him," Hallie said.

"You wouldn't. He's not from around here. We met in Vegas at a Cirque du Soleil show. We had seats next to each other. I was with a girlfriend and Teddy came with a couple of his friends. After the show they invited us to a party in Teddy's room. Things happened fast, and the following morning we got married."

"That was fast."

"You can imagine how well it worked out." Pearl gave a rueful smile. "We were already talking divorce when I found out I was pregnant. Teddy wanted me to have an abortion. I refused. Six weeks later I was single again, with full parental rights."

"Is that good or bad?" Hallie asked.

"It'd be nice if he wanted to be a part of Opal's life, but at least we avoided a custody battle."

"Does he pay child support?"

"I took a settlement check instead. I needed the money. Now I wish I'd asked for a monthly amount. Then maybe I wouldn't have to mooch off Owen."

He'd never mentioned that to Hallie. She raised her eyebrows.

"Don't get me wrong—he'd never say anything. We get along great and he's so good with Opal. But I don't like to be beholden to anyone. Owen is the same way."

Hallie gave an understanding nod. "That's why I don't take money from my parents."

They continued to talk about their lives, comfortable as if they'd never lost contact with each other.

"Are you seeing someone special?" Pearl asked.

"I'm not seeing anyone at all. You?"

Pearl shook her head. "First, I want to get back on my feet. It's cool you and Owen got to hang out for a couple days. He's such a great guy."

Hallie didn't like the speculative look in Pearl's eyes. "I learned tons from him. Our glasses are empty. Why don't I bring the wine bottle in here?"

"Sounds good."

In the living room again, Hallie refilled the glasses and Pearl went right back to her brother. "You're not seeing anyone right now. Would you go out with Owen?"

Hallie almost choked on her wine. "I don't believe he's dating much. Colleen really hurt him."

"He told you that?" Pearl seemed surprised. "He's usually close-mouthed about his personal life."

"I talked about Simon. That's probably why he opened up."

"I'm so sorry about Simon." Pearl's shoulders slumped. "I should have sent flowers instead of just a card."

"Hey, that card meant a lot. Anyway, I'm glad we reconnected."

Sometime later, after Hallie divided the last of the bottle between them, Pearl tossed her pillow aside.

"That wine was excellent, but it's all gone. I'll open another bottle."

Pearl came back with the wine and a jar of honey-roasted peanuts.

"Wanna hear a secret?" she asked, sounding a little drunk as she refilled the glasses.

Hallie nodded and her friend beckoned her closer. Although Opal was fast asleep down the hall and no one but them was in the house, Pearl lowered her voice. "Owen is convinced that neither of us has a chance at a long-lasting marriage."

Hallie frowned. "That doesn't make sense. Lots of divorced people get remarried and are happy."

"Not in our family. Our parents keep marrying and divorcing each other. Our paternal grandparents are divorced and so is our uncle. The only family members still married to each other are Geema and Big Pop."

Hallie stowed the information away. Not that it mattered. She was a long way from thinking about a relationship, let alone marriage—and by Owen's own words, so was he. Eager to move on to other things, she smiled. "Remember the time we got caught passing notes in math class?"

"How could I forget?" Pearl rolled her eyes. "Mrs. Runnels separated us for the rest of the semester. I had to sit beside Angela Harris. Boring!"

"At least she didn't put you in the front of the room. I was right under her nose and couldn't get away with anything."

The walk down memory lane continued, growing

funnier by the minute. Before long the second bottle of wine was empty and Hallie and Pearl were roaring with laughter.

~

AS OWEN HAD PREDICTED, after three straight days at the computer he saw enough light at the end of the tunnel to take Friday evening off and play poker. Tony had hosted the game, and Liam, Hank and Max had also shown up. Each man put two dollars in the kitty, with winner-take-all at the end of the evening.

The evening had been good for laughs and cut-throat competition that kept Owen on his toes. Even better, he won the kitty—a whopping ten dollars.

When the fun ended around ten-thirty, he and his buds piled out the front door into the hot, humid evening. The motion-sensor lights kicked on and the sound of cicadas filled the air.

"Tonight sucked," Max, the so-called best poker player at the station, grumbled good-naturedly.

"Speak for yourself." Owen grinned. "Beating you ranks right up there with winning last year's handball tournament."

"Don't get too cocky," Liam warned. " 'Cause next time I'm gonna whup your ass."

"See you Monday." Hank veered in the direction of his CRV.

"I'll bet Hallie was impressed when you showed up with her camera the other day." Liam all but fell over himself grinning. "How did she show her gratitude?"

Wearing a deadpan expression, Owen shrugged one shoulder. "She thanked me and I left." He ambled toward the Jag.

Max whistled. "Every time I see that beautiful car, I

picture you and some luscious babe cruising around town."

Owen grinned. "That's the plan. Later, gators."

Figuring Hallie could still be at the house, he decided to stay out for a while and check out Lucky Joe's, where a live dance band and big dance floor always drew a weekend crowd. He'd look around for a willing woman to cure him of the bad case of lust he couldn't seem to shake.

He hopped in, fired up the engine, and headed for the highway. With a crescent moon and stars studding the sky, it was a great night for a drive. Owen's wayward thoughts turned to Hallie. With her head back and her eyes closed against the wind, she'd look great in the passenger seat.

An image that made him wonder again what she'd look like in the throes of sex. And there it was, his one-thousandth woody of the week. He got so caught up fighting with himself, he forgot about Lucky Joe's and drove home.

Hallie's car was parked near the garage. Rather than open the garage door and signaling his arrival, he let the engine idle out front. Pearl hadn't drawn the drapes and light blazed through the living room window, allowing a clear view inside. She lay sprawled on the couch, gesturing animatedly, while Hallie lounged in his favorite leather chair and gestured back. The oversize seat nearly swallowed her, which was cute and for some reason sexy.

Owen considered executing a U-turn and zooming off again. Hell, no. He wasn't a randy kid with no control—he had this.

He would park in the garage, go inside, offer a quick hello and retreat to his office. So what if his intentions had been to take a break until tomorrow afternoon? Nothing wrong with changing his mind.

Distracting himself with work would push Hallie from his thoughts.

Piece of cake.

13

As soon as Owen pushed through the side door into the kitchen, he heard something that had been missing from his life for a long time—howling laughter. He couldn't help but grin. Wanting in on the joke, he headed for the living room.

He found Pearl slapping the sofa and roaring. Hallie, shaking with helpless mirth, had collapsed against the chair. On the coffee table between them were two empty wine bottles and glasses, and the jar of honey-roasted peanuts he'd picked up at the store yesterday. At most a handful or two remained.

By their startled expressions they hadn't heard him come home. "What's so funny?" he said.

His sister gave an airy wave. "We've been reminiscing about the good ol' days in high school. How was the poker game?"

"You're looking at tonight's big winner."

"How much did you win?" Hallie asked, her cheeks flushed from laughing.

"Ten bucks."

"You're rich now."

Strands of hair hung in her eyes again, driving him

nuts. Ignoring his need to tuck them behind her ears, he swiveled his head toward his sister. "You're up late."

"Am I?" She glanced at her cell phone and her eyes widened. "It's almost eleven. I had no idea. I hate to call an end to tonight, Hallie, but Opal wakes up early and I need to get some sleep."

"Of course." Hallie pushed herself out of the chair.

She was wearing a sundress, and what a dress it was. Lemon yellow with pencil-thin straps, it fit her breasts and waist like a glove before flaring at the hips. An above-the-knee skirt offered a great view of her long, bare legs, but his gaze returned to those straps, the smooth-looking skin of her shoulders and chest, and the tantalizing hint of cleavage.

Was she braless under the dress? Owen's mouth went dry. He itched to peel the straps down and find out.

Stay cool and get out of here fast.

As he gave his sister a hand up, Hallie staggered and gripped the back of the chair. "I drank more than I realized. I always have been a cheap date."

"I'm pretty wobbly myself," Pearl said. "Good thing I only have to get down the hall. You're in no shape to drive."

"I'll take you home," Owen offered.

Was he crazy? The way he felt tonight, he had no business being alone with her.

"You don't have to do that," Hallie said. "I'll call a cab."

Smart woman.

"That'll take forever," Pearl said. "Why don't you stay here and sleep in the empty guest room?"

Bad, bad idea. Spending the night under the same roof as Hallie was way too dangerous. The added

warmth in her cheeks made him wonder if she har-
bored the same thoughts.

"I'd better not. Wilbur wouldn't understand."

Pearl spread her arms and slanted Owen a look. "It
seems you'll be taking Hallie home, after all."

He was stuck, all right. Best get it over with. He
nodded to Hallie. "Ready when you are."

"Can't you come with us, Pearl?" she asked.

"Impossible—I can't leave Opal here by herself."
Owen's sister squinted at them both. "What's the
matter with you two?"

"Nothing," he replied.

"If you say so," Pearl mumbled. "Let's get together
again soon, Hallie."

"For sure."

After the two exchanged hugs Pearl headed toward
her bedroom.

In the sudden silence Hallie rubbed her arms. "I
confess, I'm a little nervous about this."

"Don't worry, I'll get you home in one piece."

"I mean us alone together."

Copy that. "Nothing to worry about. You're safe with
me," he said, both for her benefit and to remind himself.

She nodded and let out a resigned sigh. "What
about my car?"

"Tomorrow, Pearl, Opal and I will be out until after
lunch, but you can pick it up any time. I'll stow your
key under the welcome mat. You may as well give it to
me now."

Hallie hefted her purse from the end table and
dug through it for the key. "Here you go."

In silence they made their way through the
kitchen and out the side door that led to the garage.
After Owen raised the automatic door, he started to

unsnap the cover of the Jag's collapsed top so that he could put it up before backing out.

"Would you mind leaving it down?" Hallie said. "I haven't ridden in a convertible since second grade, when my dad traded his Mustang in for something 'safer,' and I sure would like to."

"It'll be windy. You'll ruin that fancy twist at the back of your hair."

"A little wind never hurt anyone."

"Don't say I didn't warn you." He hopped into his seat, reached over, and opened the passenger door. A beat later the Jag roared to life. "Buckle up and sit tight, 'cause you're in for quite a ride."

Hallie's eyes sparkled. Her dress rode halfway up her thighs. Talk about temptation. Gripping the wheel, Owen rolled out of the garage and down the driveway, then drove toward Kirkdale Road. Which was often crowded, but at this hour traffic was thin. Still, he stuck with the speed limit.

Her flouncy skirt flapped in the wind, and once or twice he caught a glimpse of white panties. After that he fixed his eyes firmly on the road.

"What are you holding back for?" she asked over the wind. "You promised me a ride."

He eyed her. "Sure you want that?"

"Absolutely."

"Suit yourself." After checking for cops and seeing none, he put the pedal to the metal.

"Wahoo!" Hallie shouted. "Faster!"

Loving her enthusiasm, he shook his head and grinned. "You're something else."

"What?"

The windshield and raised windows provided some protection against the wind, but not enough to make conversation easy. He raised his voice. "I said, you're something else. Hang on."

He upped the speed.

Her joyous expression stayed in place until he slowed and took the exit to her street. She tugged her skirt over her thighs, for all the good that did. In no time it rode up again. This time not quite up to her panties, but his imagination filled in what he could no longer see.

By the time he pulled up her driveway he was raging with need.

"That was the best car ride of my life," she said.

Most of the fancy twist had come loose. She undid what was left of it. A mess of wild curls fell almost to her shoulders.

"There's nothing like a fast convertible ride on a warm, starry night." Owen turned off the engine. "I'll walk you to the cottage."

"No need—this is the safest neighborhood around."

"After almost thirty minutes in the car I need to stretch my legs."

He opened her door and they started across the front yard. The dim porch light failed to reach them. Halfway across, Hallie lost her balance. He caught her by her bare upper arms and righted her. Her skin felt as smooth as it looked, and he caught a whiff of her lilac perfume. Under that, a womanly scent uniquely hers.

"Darned tree root," she muttered, frowning up at him.

In the darkness her eyes glittered with something that looked a lot like desire.

His body went on high alert. Too bad he'd

promised she was safe with him. He let go of her, but she wound her arms around his neck.

"You think I'm drunk, but wine has nothing to do with losing my balance. The same thing has happened several times at night in this exact spot. You'd think I'd remember about the root, but I never do."

Owen extricated himself and stepped back. "That's an easy fix—install lighting out here and have that root taken out."

Hallie snorted. "Tell that to my landlord. He can't be bothered."

"Does he realize if you or someone else got hurt, you could sue his ass?"

"I believe he has insurance for that."

"Get one of your brothers or your father to do it. They're in construction—lights and a tree root shouldn't pose a problem for them."

"Ask them for help when I've worked so hard to show my independence? No way."

"You are one stubborn woman."

Her chin jutted up. "I am not. I just want them to realize I'm capable of surviving on my own."

Owen wanted to kiss the self-righteous pucker right off her lips.

For the love of God, take her to the door, say good night, and get the hell out of here.

He nudged her forward. They were almost at the porch when she pivoted toward him. He walked smack into her.

Softness, warmth, and willing woman—his mind blanked and he forgot about keeping his word and everything else but Hallie. He hauled her up nice and close, and kissed her.

The tastes of wine and hunger filled his senses. He slid his hands to her breasts. Nope, no bra.

Her eager, breathy sounds filled the night. She thrust her chest further into his palms. Owen went up in flames. He kissed his way down her neck and lovely throat. Licked her cleavage. And reached for the straps of her dress.

Hallie pulled back to help and almost stumbled again. She'd had a lot to drink, and he wasn't about to take advantage of that.

"We have to stop," he said on a ragged breath. He positioned her straps in place and stepped back. "I promised you'd always be safe with me."

"Forget the promise. Come inside."

"You're not ready for what I want."

He let his eyes speak for him, raking his gaze slowly down her body. The low moan that tore from her throat almost brought him to his knees.

"Maybe I want the same thing."

"You drank a lot of wine. Odds are, you'll feel different in the morning." He jerked his chin at the door. "Go on in."

Instead of following her, he stood beyond the circle of light, out of reach of temptation, while she fumbled with her key. He heard Wilbur, yipping in delight.

The latch clicked open. She glanced over her shoulder at him. "Thanks for driving me home."

Before the door closed behind her, Owen was striding toward the Jag.

14

In the cottage, Hallie greeted Wilbur with a lackluster pat, plunked onto the sofa and poured out her woes to him. "I just threw myself at Owen and he tossed me back. Why did Pearl and I open that second bottle of wine?"

The lab woofed in sympathy.

"Yes, I know— he's an honorable guy. I should count myself lucky for that."

She didn't. Could a person implode from unsatisfied physical longing?

Damn the man for putting her in this state.

Hallie attempted to comb her fingers through her hair, but couldn't for the massive snarls and tangles. God only knew what she looked like. She pushed to her feet and made for the bathroom.

Standing before the vanity mirror, she stared at her reflection with horror. The curls she'd straightened this morning had become a rat's nest of ugly. She could be the poster girl for an out-of-control hair ad. Owen had warned her about riding in the convertible without a head scarf. That she hadn't listened and only now realized this proved his point—she was intoxicated.

She opened the medicine cabinet and retrieved her brush. Working it through the knots proved impossible. Copious amounts of curl relaxer helped.

How could Owen possibly want her when she looked like this?

And yet, he did.

Grooming forgotten she sank against the counter, closed her eyes and relived the steamy moments in the dark. His ravenous mouth, both demanding and giving. The fiery kisses down the side of her neck, his tongue on her skin and his big, hot hands on her breasts...

The brush clattered to the floor, putting an abrupt end to her erotic memories. Frowning, she retrieved it. Midnight was just around the corner and Wilbur never slept in. She needed to take care of her hair and get some sleep. No more thinking about Owen or his kisses.

Thanks to the relaxer her brush triumphed. She looked almost normal—at least her visible parts. Inside, she was a seething mass of desire.

Determined to ignore her feelings she changed into an old tank top and boy shorts she favored on hot summer nights. She fell into bed and turned out the lamp on the bedside table.

As always, Wilbur made himself comfy on his doggie bed nearby. He settled down right away. Hallie, not so much. Despite fatigue, the alcohol buzz, and her resolve to steer clear of all thoughts of Owen, her rebellious mind raced with possibilities and what-ifs.

Yes, he wanted her, but did that mean getting to know her better, as in dating? Or was the attraction solely about sex?

Even if they dated he'd made it clear he wasn't looking for a serious relationship. Between his parents' bad marriage and his own, Hallie didn't blame him. Or want anything deep herself. It felt too risky.

What did she want? More than a casual fling, although Hallie wasn't sure what that meant. For some reason, trying to figure it out scared her. She moved on.

The way she felt now, she was strongly tempted to toss caution to the wind and let what happened happen. Namely, satisfying the intense physical craving for Owen. But how would she feel afterward?

The nonstop questions filling her mind made her crazy. "Enough!" she ordered in the darkness. Wilbur woofed. "Go back to dreamland. I'll do the same."

Yet eager as she was to shut her brain off, sleep was a long time coming. She hugged her pillow, wishing Owen had come to bed with her, and at the same time relieved he hadn't.

~

IN WHAT SEEMED moments after Hallie fell asleep, Wilbur jumped on the bed and prodded her with his cold nose. She cracked one eye open, making her head pound, and promptly shut it. Her dry mouth tasted funny, too.

"Not yet," she croaked, pushing him away.

Refusing to be deterred, the one-track-mind dog whined and licked her face.

"Why do you have to pee so early?" Grumbling, she cupped her head between her hands, swung her legs over the mattress, and made her way gingerly to the back door. She let Wilbur out, then padded into the bathroom.

There she did the toilet thing. Splashed water on

her face. Shrugged into her robe and reached for the aspirin bottle.

After swallowing a couple tablets she called her dog in and fed him. Several cups of coffee and a slice of toast later she felt reasonably human. After a hot shower she knew she'd survive.

She wasn't so sure about living down last night. Had she really tried to jump Owen's bones?

Yep—thanks to all that wine.

Heat rose to her cheeks, making them burn. Which didn't change the fact that without a drop of alcohol in her system, she still desired him. Badly.

She also liked him more than before. The scared feeling from last night returned. Or maybe the wine had made her queasy.

At the moment she didn't have time to think about that or her brazen—and rejected—behavior. She needed to pick up her car. It was a relief Owen wouldn't be home because she wasn't ready to face him. Now to figure out how to get to his house.

With money tight she preferred not to call a cab. She wasn't about to bother Paige on a Saturday morning, and Libby had her hands full with the kids. Besides, asking her sister for a ride would only lead to questions Hallie didn't need.

Then she remembered that Millie, her closest neighbor a mile down the road, had mentioned hitting garage sales today. Last month Hallie had given her a ride or two while her car was in the shop. The woman owed her.

She called, explained she needed to pick up her sedan from a friend's house, and asked for a ride. By noon she'd retrieved her key from under Owen's welcome mat.

Not sure when he'd be back and wanting to leave

before then, she sent a quick text to Pearl, letting her know she had the car. The interior was way too hot, so Hallie opened the windows, got out, and stood in the shade until the A/C kicked in.

While she waited she admired the amazing house Owen had built. From the windows that sparkled in the sunlight to the smooth wood siding and land-scaped yard, everything appeared lovingly cared for.

For some reason her longing for him started all over again. With a sigh she returned to her car, put the windows up, and drove away.

15

"We're on our way to Geema and Big Pop's," Opal chanted in a tuneless song from her car seat.

Owen glanced at her in the rearview mirror. "That's right, graham cracker."

Still in no shape to drive, Pearl had handed Owen the keys to her compact and settled herself in the shotgun seat with a large-size commuter mug of coffee. Now she winced. "Could you please keep it down?"

Owen grinned. "Hung over?"

"A little." She adjusted her sunglasses. "Why is the sun so bright this morning?"

"It's no different than usual for the end of August. Want to borrow mine? The lenses are darker."

Pearl shook her head, then groaned. "Those aspirin had better work soon."

Owen wondered if Hallie was in the same condition. No doubt.

Some minutes later, after downing more coffee, his sister perked up. "I'm better now. I didn't hear you come back last night."

"The round-trip to Hallie's took almost an hour. You were probably out cold."

She quirked her mouth. "You sure that's what took so long?"

"Mind your own business."

He turned onto his grandparents' street and Opal squealed. "We're here!"

Owen parked in front of the house the couple had lived in for as long as he could remember.

Despite the heat, his seventy-four-year-old grandfather was working outside near a pile of wood. He took an ax to a fat log, splitting it into firewood with the vigor of a far younger man.

Opal unbuckled herself. "There's Big Pop! Let me out."

As soon as Owen did the honors his niece scrambled from the car and raced forward. Big Pop pulled off a pair of old gloves and hugged her. Owen and Pearl joined them and Pearl kissed his wizened cheek.

"Where'd all this wood come from?" Owen asked.

His grandfather mopped his forehead with a cloth from his back pocket. "The man I order my wood from dropped it by last evening and I wanted to test out the new wedge I bought at the hardware store. The rounds are green, but come winter it should be seasoned and ready."

"Why didn't you call me? I'd have come over early and given you a hand."

"I prefer to do it myself. I like the exercise."

"But I want to help." Opal hung her head.

"I'm about to stop for today, but you and I can work a few more minutes. Then I need to head inside and shower before we eat. You know where your work gloves and safety glasses are."

Opal skipped toward the shed in the back yard.

"I admire you, working when it's so darned hot outside," Pearl said.

"Doesn't bother me at all. Your Geema is inside, fixing lunch. You two go on in. Opal and I will follow shortly."

Pearl and Owen ambled into the well-loved kitchen where they'd spent so much time as kids. For as long as he could remember, his grandmother's cooking had filled the house with mouth-watering aromas, and today didn't disappoint. He sniffed appreciatively. "You made cookies."

"Chocolate chip." She tapped her cheek for a kiss. "Where's Opal?"

"Helping Big Pop with the wood." Pearl shook her head. "I can't believe he's working in this heat."

"You know your grandfather. Opal and I had a ball school-clothes shopping the other day."

"She's so excited about her new outfit and shoes." Pearl smiled. "Taking her shopping was awful sweet of you, Geema."

"My pleasure." Owen's grandmother raised her eyebrows at Owen. "Big Pop and I aren't getting any younger. We could use a few more great-grandkids."

She wanted to see him settled down with a new wife and never let an opportunity pass without reminding him. Owen stole a cookie from the cooling rack and popped the whole thing in his mouth.

"Stop that!" she scolded. "Go tell Big Pop and Opal it's almost lunchtime."

As soon as Owen's grandfather entered the house he headed upstairs to shower and change clothes. Pearl sent Opal to the powder room to wash up.

Before long they were seated at the kitchen table, enjoying cold soft drinks, tuna sandwiches, and chips.

"You're awfully quiet today, Pearl," Geema commented. "You're not eating much, either. Is your back bothering you?"

"She has a hungover," Opal said.

"Hangover," Pearl corrected. " You don't even know what that is."

"I do, too. It means you drank too much wine. Uncle Owen said so."

"A person can't get away with anything around here," Pearl muttered. "An old friend from high school came over last night. Hallie Sawyer—remember her?"

"You haven't mentioned her in ages, but I certainly do," Geema replied. "You two used to spend hours on the phone. And then she suffered that horrible tragedy."

"What's a tradegy?" Opal asked.

"Tragedy. Something very sad. Hallie lost two people she loved."

"Did she find them?"

"They're in heaven now."

"Oh." Opal's little brow wrinkled. "She didn't act sad."

"It happened a long time ago, when you were a baby," Owen said. "She's doing okay now."

His grandmother gave him a questioning look. "I didn't realize you and she were acquainted."

"She shadowed me at work for an article she's writing on firefighters."

"Is that so. I thought sure she worked at Sawyer Construction."

"She used to, but she wants to be independent."

Big Pop nodded. "As a girl that age should."

Girl? Hallie was all woman.

"Owen and Hallie get along really well," Pearl added. "He even drove her home last night."

His grandparents exchanged a cagey look. Owen rolled his eyes. "I drove her home because she and Pearl overdid the wine. I couldn't let her drive herself."

"Why didn't she spend the night? You have the room."

"She didn't want to leave her dog alone." To forestall further comments or questions, Owen stood. "I need cookies. Who's with me?"

Opal wriggled in her seat. "I am! I am!"

When most of the cookies had disappeared from the plate, Owen nodded at his sister. "Let's take care of this kitchen mess."

"What about me?" Opal asked. "I want to help, too."

"Why don't you put the napkins in the laundry basket," Geema suggested. "Then if you want, Big Pop and I will play Candy Land with you."

"Goodie!" Opal quickly did her chore, then raced for the living room, her delighted great-grandparents following.

"Thanks a heap for telling them I took Hallie home last night," Owen grumbled when he and his sister were alone.

"It's no big deal—all you did was take her home and come back." She gave him a knowing look before covering the leftover tuna and storing it in the fridge.

Ignoring her, he snagged another cookie and ate it while he loaded the dishwasher.

Turning down Hallie's invitation to come inside hadn't been easy. Her passion and eagerness turned him on big time, to the point that he was still semi-aroused.

Hell, he'd been like this since he'd first laid eyes on her at the station.

Stifling a groan, he wiped down the counter. And half-wished he'd gone back on his promise and given her what they both wanted. At least then he wouldn't be in this sorry condition.

Next time he doubted he'd show as much restraint.

And there would be a next time, when Hallie's head was clear enough to make a decision she wouldn't regret later.

Pearl's cell phone beeped, signaling a text. She slid it from her shorts pocket. "Speak of the devil—it's Hallie. She just got her car."

Owen nodded, already looking forward to seeing her again.

~

NOT LONG AFTER Hallie returned from Owen's with her car, Libby phoned. "It's been a hectic morning. I need a break from the kids and the dogs or I swear, I'll lose my mind. Chase knows I'm on the edge. He's taking them to the pool in a little while, but I need out now. Can I come over?"

Going a little crazy herself and badly in need of a distraction to take her mind off her problems, Hallie didn't even pause. "Sure, if you don't mind a walk in this heat. Wilbur needs to get out."

As soon as Libby arrived Hallie leashed the lab and they set out through the wooded area across the road. Straining forward, he sniffed and woofed and lifted his leg on half a dozen trees.

Libby adjusted her ponytail under her billed hat. "How was your evening with Pearl?"

"We had a great time. I haven't laughed that much in I don't know how long. I got to meet her daughter, Opal. She's adorable."

"So Pearl is married?"

"Divorced."

Libby nodded. "Where does she live?"

Hallie wanted to skip right over that. Too late. Nothing to do but tell the truth. "Actually, they're staying with Owen." She explained about Pearl's accident and the new job that started next week. "Once she saves enough money for her own place, she and Opal will move out," she finished.

"It's good that she can work again. Did Owen hang out with you?"

The innocent-sounding question would only lead to others. Hallie hesitated.

"He did." Libby looked all too pleased.

Hallie hurried to correct her. "Actually, he was out most of the evening. He didn't come home until Pearl and I had finished a couple bottles of wine. I was in no shape to get behind the wheel so he drove me home. In his Jaguar. With the top down."

"Nice. I assume he drove your car back this morning?"

"No. He and Pearl had to be someplace. I caught a ride to his house with Millie and picked it up."

Libby looked hurt. "Why didn't you ask me?"

"Because when you called last night you reminded me how busy your Saturdays are."

"If you'd needed something, Chase would have stepped in sooner."

"And I was supposed to know that how?"

"What I mean is, I'm your sister and I'm here for you."

"I appreciate that." Hallie made a snap decision. "If I tell you what happened when Owen took me home, do you swear not to tell a soul? Not even Chase?"

"My lips are sealed." All eyes, Libby leaned in.

"Owen walked me to the door, which was sweet but completely unnecessary. On the way, I tripped on that stupid tree root."

"Again? You ought to ask Joe or Brett to remove it."

"I'd rather not."

"Come on, Hallie, it's a hazard and needs to go. They won't charge you."

"That's not the point and you know it." Hallie eyed her sister. "Do you want to hear what happened or not?"

Libby shut her mouth.

"I kissed him. Actually, he kissed me."

"You and Owen Ayers kissed." Libby's eyebrows disappeared under her bangs. "Wow."

"You can say that again. It was even better than the first time."

"You kissed him before? You've been holding out on me, you sneak."

"I'm not holding back now." Hallie sucked in a breath, blew it out, and plunged ahead. "The evening didn't end so well. I made a complete fool of myself and invited him inside. I wanted to make love."

Her sister gave a well-of-course nod. "I don't blame you. It's been a long time for you and he's a hot guy."

"True, only remember, I wasn't exactly sober. If I had been... You know how I feel about casual sex."

"You're only human, Hallie. You have needs. I see nothing wrong with bending your own rules now and then."

Didn't Paige say the same thing? "It's not about rules, it's about getting to know someone first," Hallie explained. "I'm not sure Owen wants that."

She did. There went her stomach again. From now on, she would limit herself to one glass of wine.

Libby frowned. "You look so unhappy."

"I was thinking about last night when he refused my offer. He doesn't want me to regret anything later."

"He wouldn't have done that if he was interested only in sex."

A possibility Hallie hadn't considered. "Or maybe

pleading with him to take me to bed turned him off. I'm so embarrassed."

"You'll get over it. I'll bet Owen already has. You'll find out when you talk."

"If we talk. It's not like we're dating. All he did was drive me home." And add fuel to the fire inside her.

Libby's cell phone rang. She checked the screen. "It's Chase."

While she conferred with her husband, Wilbur jerked Hallie toward yet another tree. He finished christening the trunk just about the time Libby disconnected.

"The trip to the pool was a disaster," she said. "Reese got stung by a bee, Bella slipped and skinned her knee, and Jimmy won't stop crying. Now Chase is about to lose his sanity. I have to get home."

"You could always hide out here instead," Hallie said on the walk back. "I can make lemonade."

"I wish I could stay. Rain check. Keep me posted on Owen. I hope he calls."

"Time will tell." Hallie pulled her sister into a warm hug. "See you tomorrow at Sunday dinner."

16

"Thanks for not mentioning you know what," Hallie murmured as she and Libby cleared the table Sunday evening.

In the middle of a conversation with her father, Hallie's mother narrowed her eyes. "I don't know what. Why don't you tell me?"

Eavesdropping much? Hallie wide-eyed her. "I don't know how you even heard me, Mom."

"Sometimes a whisper is louder than a yell."

"We were discussing the magazine article for Fire Prevention magazine," Hallie said. "I'm working on the final draft and hope to send it off next week. I didn't want to mention it because I'm not in the mood for a lecture on what you think I should do with my life instead."

So she'd told a tiny, little fib. Her mother didn't need to know about Owen.

Not buying in, her mother snorted. "That is not what you and Libby were whispering about."

"It's nothing," Libby assured her. "Just sister stuff."

~

AN EARLY MORNING fire at a downtown drycleaner's started Tuesday with a bang. Owen and his crewmates were setting the fire engine to rights afterward when Miranda broke in over the intercom. "Phone call for Owen, line two."

Family and friends contacted him through his cell phone. Must be a business call. Scratching his head, he headed upstairs to the kitchen area where it was quieter and picked up. "Owen Ayers."

"Hello there," cooed a female voice he didn't recognize.

"Uh, hi. Who is this?"

"Erica."

Owen frowned and tried to place her. "Who?"

"We met at the teacher safety training? I gave you my number?"

Now he remembered—the blonde. "If you're calling to schedule a fire safety workshop for your students, you need to speak with Hank Gardener. His card is in the packet I handed out, but let me give you his contact information again."

"That's not why I'm calling. Do you want to get together for drinks Friday night?"

Owen wasn't even tempted. Hallie was the woman he wanted. His thoughts went no further than that. "Can't make it," he said.

"You're still involved with the woman who came with you to the training. What a shame. If anything changes, you have my number."

Nope, but he wasn't going to correct her. He hung up and returned to the apparatus bay.

17

After the umpteenth read-through of the Fire Prevention magazine article, Hallie said a little prayer and hit the "send" button. She so wanted John Bodine to like her article about the Guff's Lake Fire Department. No, she wanted him to love it and give her the go-ahead to write the series.

If that happened, who knew—the magazine might begin accepting her work on a regular basis. Or hire her to write feature articles.

A few other magazines consistently bought her pieces, but in order to have a steady income stream she needed more. Assignments from multiple sources with payments she could count on? Yes, please. Dizzy with the possibilities, she sat back and grinned.

An insidious thought crept in. What if John didn't like the piece and failed to okay the series or any future pieces?

Bye-bye smile and hello anxious, queasy stomach. Facing the unknown was always a little scary. Although lately her stomach had been like this a lot. She hadn't felt normal since before her Friday night wine fiasco.

While she pondered that, Wilbur, ever attuned to

her moods, whined, put his head in her lap and gazed at her with mournful eyes.

No point in getting worked up over something she couldn't control. Mr. Bodine's decision was out of her hands. "Don't you worry," she told the lab. "I'll drum up ideas for the magazines that know and like my work, and everything will be fine."

Back to Friday night. She hadn't heard a word from Owen since then, not even a text or an email. Throwing herself at him had definitely doused his interest, and his silence spoke loud and clear. He didn't want to get to know her better.

How disappointing, but at least she knew where things stood. The instant the thought entered her mind the tension in her stomach eased. Weird—or maybe not.

She was afraid of getting involved with Owen. Similar to how Paige had felt about Milo. Except Milo and Paige had fallen in love from the get-go. Owen didn't want a relationship at all. According to Hallie's stomach, neither did she.

She gave her dog one more pat and pushed him away. "I guess we won't be seeing Owen again, but it's for the best."

Except for one little problem. She wanted him, wanted his mouth and hands on her everywhere. Her nipples tightened and a needy ache started low in her body.

Stop it!

She grabbed her phone and texted Paige and Libby.

Just sent the article, 2 days early!

WTG! Libby replied.

Way to impress your editor! Paige texted. We need to get together soon and catch up.

And how. Hallie hadn't talked to her friend since before Owen had turned her world upside down with kisses and more... But she wasn't going to think about that.

She jumped up. "I haven't touched the garden in ages and the weeds are out of control, and you could do with some exercise," she told the dog. "Let me change and we'll do some gardening."

Moments later, in an oversize T-shirt, old cutoffs, and a faded sun visor, Hallie slid her feet into flip-flops and headed out the door.

August had come and gone in a blink. Despite the warm September afternoon, the faint whiff of fall hung in the air. Thrilled to be outside, Wilbur raced around the fenced yard, barking at birds and chasing squirrels.

Hallie was on her knees pulling weeds, which turned out to be terrific therapy for a sexually frustrated woman destined to stay that way for a while, when the dog gave his company-yippee! woof.

In the distance, Owen's bronze Jag convertible tooled up the road. Her heart lifted in her chest. "Traitor," she told it.

Irritated with herself and mad at Owen for his days of silence, she scrambled to her feet. She barely had time to wonder what had brought him here before he turned up her driveway and pulled to a stop.

She was about to find out.

~

HALLIE STOOD at the edge of a flowerbed, her gloved hands on her hips and her long legs looking oh so fine in tattered cutoffs that barely peeked from under her oversize "Pink in Concert" T-shirt. Unlike the grinning dog racing to meet him, she didn't crack a smile or start forward. She didn't seem at all happy he'd come.

"Hi," he said, pausing to rub the lab's head. "Your garden is lookin' good."

She pushed her sun visor back a fraction and narrowed her eyes. If looks could kill...

Somehow he'd made her unhappy. Clueless, he eyed her. "What'd I do?"

"If you think you can stop by any old time without so much as a text message since the last time I saw you, you're mistaken."

It hadn't even been a week. How was he to know she expected him to contact her right away? When it came to women, he never had been the sharpest chip in the computer. "I haven't had time," he said. "I spent Saturday morning with my grandparents. The rest of the weekend I was holed up in my office, working on the training program, and for the last forty-eight hours I've been at the station. I'm here now."

The contrary tilt of her chin and her compressed lips told him what she thought of that. Owen took a stab at what might have upset her. "If this is about the other night, let's talk."

"Just tell me why you stopped by."

Because he needed to see her the way he needed something sweet after a meal. Also to help her out. "Your front yard is dangerous at night," he said. "The landlord isn't going to do anything to fix the problem, and you won't ask your family. That's why I'm here— to take you to the hardware store, find lighting and install it."

Her wary expression eased. "You'd do that for me?"

"Yeah. I don't want you tripping on that tree root and breaking your neck."

"On that we agree." Hallie tugged off her gloves. "I guess we should talk."

She led him to a pair of redwood patio chairs and they both sat down. For a pleasant few seconds he got lost in the way she crossed one tan leg over the other. Then she cleared her throat and he shifted his focus upward.

"I'm embarrassed by how I acted that night," she said. "I've never pushed myself at a man before."

"You overdid the wine—no big deal. Consider it forgotten."

Right, and he was Luke Skywalker. Owen remembered the taste of her hunger and the catch in her breath when he touched her. The soft weight of her breasts in his hands, her lush curves tight against him...

It was all he could do not to reach for her and pull her close for a repeat. Good thing she couldn't read minds.

"Well, I haven't forgotten." Her golden-brown eyes warmed before she glanced away. When she turned back to him the warmth had all but disappeared. "Maybe we should stay away from each other."

Hadn't seen that coming. "Because we almost crossed the line? Give me some credit, Hallie. I promised you'd be safe with me. As tempted as I was to break my word—and you'd tempt a saint—I kept it."

"Yes, you did." Solemn-faced, she adjusted the sun visor and muttered something about telling the truth. "The alcohol made me bold, but I didn't feel any different the next morning, Owen. I still don't."

Copy that and ditto.

"I haven't wanted a man physically since I lost Simon. Then you came along." She swallowed. "I think two people should get to know each other before they become physically intimate, but when I'm with you... I feel things that scare me. Now you know."

Whoa. She deserved the same level of honesty from him—fair play and all that. "I think we're getting to know each other pretty well. As much as I like you and as bad as I want you, I never want to hurt you. It bears repeating that I'm in no shape to get into a committed relationship. Sometimes I wonder if I ever will be."

"Yes, I remember. Nothing has changed for me, either. I'm nowhere near ready for love."

Who'd said anything about that? "Don't confuse love with sex," he cautioned.

Her eyes widened as if startled. Something hot and powerful arced between them and he knew they weren't finished by a long shot.

But she might feel differently.

"I can either leave right now or take you to the hardware store—which will it be?" He sucked in a breath and waited.

Making up her mind took several agonizing moments. Finally she nodded. "I'll go to the hardware store with you. Give me five minutes to put Wilbur inside, change, and find a scarf for my hair. I'll meet you out here."

Owen exhaled in relief.

18

As Hallie exchanged her gardening clothes for an outfit she could wear in public, she reviewed the conversation with Owen. Specifically the part about confusing sex with love. Did she do that? She thought back to the relationships she'd had, including the one with Simon.

The answer was clear: she definitely equated the two. Somehow she'd never realized that, not even when discussing the subject with Paige or Libby. As intelligent as they both were they'd never pointed this out. Which made Owen's insight all the more amazing. He might be the smartest person she'd ever met.

Now that her eyes had been opened, her view of things shifted. She and Owen didn't have to be in love for her to enjoy sex. That they liked each other was enough. She could satisfy her physical hunger for him without tapping into the deeper feelings she wasn't ready for.

That felt safe and right. Elated, she braided her hair to protect it from turning into a bird's nest of tangles.

And yet.

The thought of making love with him unsettled

her. "Four years without a man is a long time," she reasoned. "Anyone would be nervous."

With that, she made up her mind. At some point this afternoon she would tell Owen she wanted to continue to see him after all, and that she also wanted sex.

~

RIDING in Owen's Jag in broad daylight was almost as fun as a moonlight drive. Hallie couldn't wipe the smile from her face. "Opal started kindergarten today, right?" she said over the wind.

He nodded. "Pearl dropped her off on the way to her new job. Big changes for them. How's the article going?"

"I sent it off today."

"Good for you."

"Are you making any progress on your training program?"

"Getting there. If all goes well, it'll be in my beta testers' capable hands by tomorrow."

Hallie was impressed. "Shouldn't you be at home, finishing up?"

"I have the whole evening and all night for that."

"Okay. What's a beta tester?"

"A person who runs through the system and makes sure everything works as it should. I hired three of them, and they're top-notch. Fast, too."

"I hope your program is perfect."

"You and me both, but that never happens."

"It's awful nice of you to do this for me."

"Like I said, setting you up with lights is important."

She went all warm and fuzzy inside. "You are so thoughtful."

"Me?" He seemed surprised. "I've been called a lot of things, but never that."

"Like what?"

"Distant and out of touch with my feelings."

He shrugged as if the words meant nothing to him. Hallie suspected they hurt. "Who would say that?"

"Who do you think? Colleen."

He sped up as if trying to outrace the labels, the wind drowning out further conversation. With the sun warm on Hallie's face and the scenery flying past, who could think about anything but the joy of riding in the convertible with the hottest man around?

She pinched herself to make sure she wasn't dreaming. But no, she was wide awake and alive, her senses fully attuned to the here and now and her body doing its familiar tingle.

By the time Owen slowed the Jag to a more sedate speed and took the exit leading to the hardware store, she was as aroused as the night he'd taken her home.

Before she lost her nerve she broached the subject foremost in her thoughts. "I want to keep seeing you, Owen."

"Yeah?" A slow grin lit his face. "What changed your mind?"

"What you said about not confusing sex with love makes a lot of sense. We can be together without loving each other."

His veiled look was impossible to read.

He signaled and turned into the General Hardware parking lot. Instead of finding a slot close to the entrance he pulled into the far corner of the deserted back row. He shut off the engine and turned to her.

"Let me get this straight. For the first time in years you're interested in getting physical and you want to do that with me—without any expectations of a serious relationship."

"Yes." He was quiet so long, she began to wonder. "If you changed your mind..." She just might die.

"Make no mistake, Hallie—I want you."

The combination of his blazing eyes and intimate tone went straight to her most sensitive body part. She pressed her thighs together.

Then why was he hesitating?

"Sex is a big deal," he said as if he'd read her mind. "You went from scared to ready awful fast. I don't want you to do something you'll regret later."

"That's what you said the night I drank too much wine."

"And it still stands. Better to wait until you're one hundred percent sure."

She tugged off the scarf, absently checked her braid, and decided he had a point. As badly as she ached to make love, she wasn't quite there yet. A little more time couldn't hurt. "I agree with you, Owen—we should wait awhile. But that doesn't mean we have to keep our hands off each other."

"I don't have a problem with that."

He leaned across the gear shift between the seats, grasped her head in his warm palms and kissed her. Long, deep, and oh, so good.

A blaring horn followed by, "Get a room!" ended the delicious moment.

With her lips burning and her body aroused, Hallie could barely focus. "You don't make it easy for a girl to go slow."

Owen sat back. "That's a taste of what's in store for you when you're finally ready. Now, let's get those yard lights."

19

Wowed by Hallie's enthusiastic response in the Jag moments earlier, Owen had trouble keeping his hands off her. But touching her was dangerous, especially in the middle of the hardware store parking lot.

God above, he wanted to make love with her. Waiting until she was sure she wanted the same thing would be sheer hell—but worth the wait.

Inside, the store teemed with people.

"For a Wednesday afternoon this place is packed," Hallie commented over the hum of conversation and beeping payment registers.

"Blame the back to school specials. You won't find school supplies here, but like all the other retailers they want in on the action."

"I wonder where we can find the outdoor lighting," she said.

"In the rear of the store, against the wall." On the way there, he lifted a flyer from a rotating stand and gave it to her. "Check this out for coupons."

"I will. How do you know where the lighting is?"

"This has always been my grandfather's go-to place for household supplies. He liked to bring me along when I was a kid. Then when I built my place, I came here to pick out the fixtures and lights."

"He's your Big Pop, right? You gave him the name when you were little."

Owen eyeballed her. "Where did you hear that?"

"Pearl."

No knowing what all his sister might have said. "What else did she tell you about me?"

"Let's see... You're good to her and you're a terrific uncle to Opal."

Nothing too heavy, then. He grinned. "She's good to me, too. Find any coupons?"

Hallie studied the flyer. "Here's one for fifteen percent off on any purchase of twenty dollars or more, including sale items."

"Excellent. Turn left and we're there."

As Owen had figured, most of the lights in the store had been marked down.

Hallie's face lit up. "With the sale prices and the coupon, I can't lose."

After browsing the displays she pointed at a five-foot pole with single lantern-style light at the top. "What about this?"

Owen scanned the card describing the item. "Installation would involve digging up the yard and tapping into the existing power source. That could cost big bucks, and if your landlord won't reimburse you..."

"He won't." She sighed. "I can't afford anything too pricey. Maybe we should forget this."

"Don't give up so fast." Owen nodded to a shelf of solar-powered lights. "These shouldn't cost much."

Hallie looked through the selection and settled on a modest set of six-inch-high lights. "Will these work?"

"Probably. Let me check with Rafe. He knows a lot about lighting."

As Owen dug his phone from his pocket, Hallie froze. She leaned in and spoke in a barely audible voice. "Hold off on that call for a minute. I think I hear my mom in the next aisle over."

"And that's bad?" he said for her ears only.

"You don't know her. If she sees me with you, I'll never hear the end of it."

"My Geema's the same way." Owen glanced around, grabbed Hallie's hand, and pulled her behind a large display of light bulbs.

She giggled. "Ssh," he cautioned, laying his finger against her lips.

With a mischievous twinkle in her eyes, she caught his fingertip lightly between her teeth and drew it into her mouth.

Owen imagined her doing the same thing with a different part of his body and quickly extracted his finger.

"Did that hurt?" she asked in her normal voice.

"Not exactly." He nodded at the hard-on straining his fly.

"Oh. Oops."

A woman with Hallie's eyes and coloring poked her head behind the display. "Hallie! I thought I heard your voice. What are you doing back here, and what happened to your hair?"

"Um, hi, Mom." Blushing, Hallie stepped away from Owen and touched her head. "What's wrong with it?"

"Your braid is cockeyed and you look ruffled." The woman's smile reminded Owen of the Cheshire cat in Alice and Wonderland.

"Owen has a convertible. I wore a scarf, but the wind..." Hallie shrugged.

Her mom glanced curiously at him. "My daughter

seems to have forgotten her manners. I'm Sandy Sawyer."

Owen extended his hand. "Owen Ayers. Pleased to meet you, Mrs. Sawyer."

"You're the firefighter from the calendar, the man who showed Hallie around the fire station."

"That's right."

"I didn't realize she was still shadowing you. Although you're not in uniform today."

"Owen's off right now. He offered to—"

Mrs. Sawyer's cell phone rang, cutting Hallie off. She glanced at the screen. "It's your father. I'd better take this or he'll keep calling until I answer. Nice to meet you, Owen. See you at dinner Sunday, Hallie."

She pivoted and walked off, her voice carrying easily. "Hi, honey. I'm at the hardware store. I just ran into Hallie and you won't believe who she's here with."

"I'll never live this down," Hallie muttered.

"What's to live down? We're at the hardware store."

"Hiding behind a display."

"Your mom probably didn't even notice."

"Trust me, she notices everything."

"She seemed okay to me."

"You haven't sat through dinner with her, my dad, and my grandparents. All pushing me to start dating again. I don't know what they'll think now."

"If it gets them off your back, what's the harm?"

"I don't want them getting any ideas and I'm sure you don't, either. You were going to call Rafe."

"Right." After a brief conversation with his crewmate, Owen shared what he'd learned. "Installing these should be a piece of cake. Rafe has a lot going on and won't be able to give me a hand, but Hank and Max should be available."

"Tell them I'll reward them with beer and Harvey's pizza."

Best pizza in town. Owen licked his lips. "Who could turn that down?"

"Are you planning to do this now?"

He shook his head. "Tomorrow afternoon. I have something else in mind for us today." He didn't hide his meaning.

Understanding softened her features and her lips parted just enough to invite a kiss. Owen could hardly wait to get her home. He nudged her forward. "Let's get out of here."

"What time tomorrow are you thinking?" she asked as they made their way to the checkout area up front. "Because mid-afternoon I have an appointment to take my car in for its fifty-thousand mile tune-up. I may not get back until almost dinnertime."

"You don't have to be there. Leave me a key and show me where to find the electrical panel in case I need it. As soon as I talk with Hank and Max, I'll text and let you know when we'll be there."

"That'll work. I'll pick up the pizza on my way home. What toppings do you want?"

"Extra large with the works. Better get two pies."

Hallie frowned. "Is it my imagination, or was the older couple we just passed staring at us? So is that woman with the toddler over there. My hair must be a real mess." She dug in her purse for a mirror and directed a critical look at herself. "It's not that bad." She retied the braid and smoothed a few errant wisps. "Are people looking at us, or am I paranoid?"

"They're looking, all right. Blame the calendar."

"The calendar—of course. You're famous."

Owen rolled his eyes. Even the checker, a teenage girl he'd never laid eyes on, checked him out. Hallie, too, and she fixed them both with a knowing look. Huh.

"Drive around to the delivery area," she said. "They'll have your order ready."

In short order Owen had stowed the lights in the Jag's rear trunk. He started the engine, turned out of the lot, and sped toward Hallie's place.

ON THE DRIVE HOME, Hallie barely noticed the wind or the scenery flying by. She was too caught up in what would happen in the privacy of the cottage.

"Where do you want these lights?" Owen asked as he pulled into the driveway.

She didn't care where he put them, as long as it didn't take long. "There's room in the carport."

"What about the electrical panel?"

"In the laundry room off the kitchen."

He nodded. "You go in. I'll follow shortly."

Wilbur greeted her, then pressed his nose to the screen door and whined for Owen. "We both need to be patient," Hallie said. "It won't be long."

She hurried into the bathroom to brush her teeth. When Owen tromped inside, Wilbur woofed and danced with glee. He seemed to like Owen as much as Hallie did.

"I have snacks and pop," she offered. "Are you hungry?"

"Not for food." His smoldering look could have liquefied steel.

Weak with need, she crooked her finger at him. "Come over here, you."

With lightning speed he complied, locking his

arms around her. He took her mouth with a bruising hunger that left her breathless.

"More," she managed.

"We're on the same page again." He pulled her into another searing kiss and backed her toward the living room.

Hallie resisted. "Couldn't we go to my bedroom instead?"

"We talked about that. Not yet."

"But I—"

He tugged her onto the couch and she forgot what she'd tried to say. Her senses filled with the man in her arms. His smell, his taste, his strength.

"Touch me," she whispered, guiding his hands to her breasts.

Letting out a growl of pleasure, he traced her swollen nipples with his thumbs.

A moan filled the air. Hers, she dimly realized.

Somehow both their shirts disappeared. His chest was every bit as magnificent as she'd imagined—a smattering of dark hair on his muscled pecs, and smooth, hard abs.

Beauty-wise she couldn't begin to compete. If only she'd worn her lacy demi-bra...

That was her last thought before her mind blanked and sensation took over. Her bare back against the corduroy cushions. Owen's mouth tasting her through the bra.

It wasn't enough. She pulled back and reached behind her. "Let me take this off."

"I'll do it." Seconds later, he tossed the bra aside. He studied her through slitted eyes. "Damn, you're pretty."

He cupped her breasts with a reverence that made

her feel beautiful. Half on top of her, he again took her mouth.

Skin on skin. Hallie savored the rasp of his chest hair against her nipples. His thigh between hers. In a silent plea for more she threw her head back and arched up.

His tongue flicked across her nipples. Half out of her mind, she writhed under him. "Please, Owen."

"Tell me what you want."

"Go lower. Between my legs."

His hot palm slid down her stomach. He unhooked the clasp on her shorts, pulled on the zipper. Hallie sucked in a breath she didn't release until he delved inside her panties and found her most sensitive place. Right. There. Heaven.

He knew just how to touch her. The world shrank to that one small nub of connection and pleasure.

"You're nice and wet," he said.

"Because..." she could barely speak. "Because I want you. Oh, God, Owen, I'm about to climax."

"Do it, Hallie. Let go."

He did something amazing with his fingers that pushed her over the edge. She shattered.

She'd barely returned to the here and now before Owen swore and sat up.

"What's wrong?" she asked.

"You're crying."

She was? Hallie touched her cheeks and found them wet.

His face shuttered, Owen retrieved her bra and top, then gave her a hand up. Confused, she covered herself with her clothes and headed for the bathroom to dress and try to make sense of her response.

20

Hallie studied herself in the bathroom mirror. Glowing skin, pink-tinged lips—and watery eyes.

Where did they come from? She'd never reacted this way before. Puzzled, she searched her heart. She wasn't at all sad. The opposite, in fact. This afternoon a part of her that had been closed off for a long time had opened—thanks to Owen.

Helping her with the lights because he didn't want her to hurt herself, not rushing her into sex... What a great guy. Generous, too. Touching her without asking for anything in return, giving her such pleasure. She'd so needed that.

The release alone had been enough to bring her to tears. That's why she'd cried.

But not the whole reason. The powerful emotions that had deluged her had also played a part. Gratitude, warmth, and something else. Feelings for Owen, strong feelings. She liked him a lot, even more than she'd realized. More than was smart.

Not love, she hastily assured herself—for all the good that did. Her stomach lapsed into a tense, scared knot, but she wanted him too much to give in to fear.

Besides, liking him was not the same as loving him.

Owen is a prince of a guy and I want more of what we just did—that's all. She visualized putting a lock on her heart to protect herself, and to her relief the tension inside ebbed into a vague twinge.

After splashing water on her face and fixing her hair and makeup she felt better. Except for one thing. If Owen had any inkling of her growing feelings he'd light out of her life so fast...

Hallie refused to let that happen. When she explained the reason for her tears, she'd skip right over the part about her feelings. That'd work. She reached for the door to rejoin Owen.

OWEN PULLED on his T-shirt and waited for Hallie to come out of the bathroom. She'd been in there a long time. That couldn't be good.

"You okay?" he called out.

"I need a minute."

She claimed she wanted sex, but this proved she wasn't ready. What had he been thinking, getting hot and heavy so soon?

Thinking? When he and Hallie fooled around, his brain left the premises.

She'd enjoyed it, too—or had seemed to. Before the tears of regret.

Seriously pissed off at himself for his lack of control he paced the little living room and called himself a few choice names. Impatient jackass, insensitive jerk, idiot.

Whining softly, Wilbur butted his leg and gazed

up at him with mournful eyes. Owen rubbed behind the lab's ears. "Thanks for the condolences, pal."

At last the bathroom door clicked open. Hallie returned to the living room with her hair freshly braided and her clothes in place. At a loss what to expect, he kept his expression neutral.

Her eyes were dry and clear and she didn't seem upset anymore. She looked like her normal self—except for her slightly swollen lips and flushed skin.

So beautiful.

Owen wanted her something awful. Which made him the biggest dog around. No offense to you, Wilbur.

"Did I hear you pacing?" she asked.

"I do that sometimes."

"Owen, I—"

Needing to speak his piece first, he held up his hands and silenced her. "I know things moved too fast. My fault—I got carried away."

"You didn't do anything I didn't want."

"Except make you cry." He raked his fingers over his buzz cut. "I feel bad about that, but I won't lie—I'm not sorry for anything that happened. If you want to slap me, go ahead."

Setting his jaw he braced for the angry sting.

"I don't want to slap you, and I'm not sorry, either. I liked what we did—a lot."

Her eyes went soft and unfocused like they did when he touched her. Underneath, he glimpsed something deeper. Warning bells clanged in his head.

She cared way too much. That changed everything. He shoved his hands in his pockets. "We both enjoyed ourselves, but I don't think we should fool around anymore."

Hallie looked bewildered. "I don't understand."

"I know you have feelings for me. I don't want you to get hurt."

"Of course I do, Owen. I like you, but that's as far as it goes."

He suspected she was lying. "You sure?"

"What kind of question is that?" Scoffing, she settled her hands on her hips. "Give me some credit. I want this, and I'm going in with my eyes wide open. Why don't you believe me?"

"I saw your tears."

"You drew the wrong conclusion. They were part of the release I felt from my climax —my first in four years."

Certain he'd misheard, he squinted at her. "In all that time you never satisfied yourself?"

"I know it sounds strange, but I wasn't interested. I'm very interested now—with you."

He desired her more than he'd wanted anyone in a long time. That and the fact that she looked him straight in the eyes outweighed any misgivings convinced him. "I guess we're okay."

"Better than okay." She smiled sweetly.

Relieved, he grinned. "Told you we'd be good together."

She walked him to the door. "I'll take Wilbur with me so he won't bother you if you need to get into the cottage while I'm gone tomorrow. I'll leave a spare key under the paint can in the carport."

"Copy that." He kissed her gently and left.

Four crumpled beer cans, two empty, extra-large pizza boxes, and a flattened box of what had held bakery cookies littered Hallie's coffee table. She shook her head. "I've never seen three men inhale food the way you did."

With only room enough for two at her kitchen table, she'd served dinner in the living room. Max and Hank had the chairs and Owen sat beside her on the couch.

He gave an unapologetic grin. "We were hungry."

"Not anymore," Hank said with a contented sigh.

"Couldn't eat another bite." Max patted his still-flat stomach.

Despite having consumed what had to be a zillion calories, none of them had so much as a rounded belly. "I'll bet you never put on weight no matter what you eat," she guessed. Whereas she gained a pound just thinking about food. "It's so unfair."

Owen's avid gaze flickered over her. "You look perfect to me."

She resisted the urge to slide over and kiss him in front of his friends. "You guys are the best. I love my new solar-powered lights—or I will, once they start working."

"According to the directions, the solar panel that fuels the lights will be fully charged by dusk tomorrow." Owen stood and nodded to his crewmates. "Don't you need to get back?"

He seemed in a big hurry to get rid of them. But then, Hallie felt the same.

As soon as they brought their plates and garbage into the kitchen, he hustled them out.

"I enjoyed that," Hallie said when they'd gone. "They're such nice guys."

"Yeah. What are you doing all the way over there?"

"I'm only a few feet away."

"Much too far."

He tugged her close and kissed her. She sank against him.

When they finally came up for air, he rested his forehead against hers. "I've been waiting all day for that."

As had she. She tried to pull him into another kiss.

"Not so fast. This kitchen won't clean itself."

"There isn't much to do, but if it'll make you feel better..."

"It will. I'll take the trash out to the garbage bin." He whistled for Wilbur. "Come with me and do your business."

Happy to comply, the dog followed him out.

Smiling, Hallie loaded the dishwasher.

When Owen reentered the kitchen with the lab, he asked for the broom.

"Have you always been this neat and tidy?" she asked while he swept the floor.

"For as long as I can remember. If Pearl and I didn't clean the house, it didn't get done."

Hallie nodded. "Chores. I had them, too. That's how I earned my allowance."

"We did all the housework and didn't get paid a dime."

"Your parents couldn't afford it?"

"They never thought about it. Too busy fighting or in the bedroom with the door locked."

"So you played the adult."

"Pretty much. Hand me the dust pan."

Hallie couldn't imagine what that must have been like. As busy as her parents were, they'd always been in charge and had never ignored her or her siblings. Once again, she was grateful for her carefree childhood. "That can't have been fun."

"It was what it was. I always had an easier time at my grandparents'. Anyway, knowing how to keep a clean place helped prepare me for my job at the station. I'll put the broom and dust pan away."

He didn't seem at all bitter about his childhood. Her admiration for him upped another notch.

Was there anything she didn't like about this man? It would be so easy to fall for him. Good thing she'd locked her heart up.

"Owen, do you know Betty Randall?" she asked when he returned.

"The biggest gossip in town?" He rolled his eyes. "Who doesn't."

"I ran into her when I had the car serviced this afternoon. She was leaving as I came in and gave me such a look."

"Like what?"

Hallie had to think a minute. "Sly and knowing, as if she had a secret."

"No doubt she expected you to ask about it."

"I wanted to, but the mechanic came over to talk about my car. By the time he finished she'd left."

"Sooner or later you're bound to hear about it. Wanna go in the living room and fool around?"

"That depends, Mr. Ayers. What do you have in mind?"

"Lots of stuff. For starters, learning more about pleasuring you. What you especially like and what makes you squirm."

He ran his finger lightly across Hallie's nipple. She moaned. "You're making me squirm right now."

His low laugh washed over her. "It's good to know I'm on the right track."

ON HIS WAY to the door much later, Owen slung his arm around Hallie. She fit well against him, her head in the hollow of his shoulder and her arm around his waist. Her hair was loose and wild, and the taste and smell of her lingered on his tongue.

"You're impossible to resist," he growled, backing her against the wall for one more mind-numbing kiss.

The breathy sound he'd begun to crave shuddered from her lips. When they finally broke apart, hunger etched her features.

Keeping his need in check wasn't easy, but he was a patient man. He would wait until Hallie knew for sure that she was ready to make love.

He tucked her bangs behind her ears. "I expect to hear from my beta testers sometime tomorrow."

"You said they were fast, but that's really fast."

"And they're well-compensated for it. I'll need to fix whatever problems they find, then run through another test. The finished product has to go out a week from Monday. What I mean is, you won't see or hear from me for a while."

"Got it. Good luck." She opened the door.

Whistling, he headed for the Jag. As it purred to life he cast one last glance at her. Standing in the doorway with light from the cottage spilling around her and that wild hair, she looked like a goddess.

His—for now.

22

Knowing she wouldn't see Owen for more than a week put Hallie in a gloomy mood. But she understood deadlines and his was looming. Never mind, she had plenty to distract her. Writing projects, gardening, laundry, cleaning, and running errands.

Thinking positive and wanting to be prepared when John Bodine approved her series idea, she pored over her list of fire departments in towns of similar size to Guff's Lake. She'd found hundreds around the country but she only needed three. Narrowing the list wasn't easy and took several hours, but she managed to select her top choices and several alternates just in case.

She bought groceries. Took Wilbur to the dog park twice and enjoyed afternoon walks with him through the woods. She decided to start a new knitting project, an afghan for the cold winter nights ahead. That meant a trip to Deb's Knitting Store for a pattern and yarn.

Sunday morning she plugged her iPod into speakers and cranked up an Adele album. Sitting cross-legged on the couch and humming along, she pulled out a length of yarn and set to work. She was supposed to count stitches. Instead she fantasized about Owen. Touching her, tasting her, making her wild...

Hallie shifted restlessly and pulled out the stitches. Two more attempts and failures later she admitted defeat. How could she concentrate when all she wanted was to be with Owen? Really be with him.

To make love.

She could hardly wait to tell Owen, but didn't want to distract him while he was racing to finish his work. She called Paige.

"Hi, there," Hallie's friend answered in a pleased voice. "It's been weeks."

"I know. A lot has happened since we last touched base."

"Don't tell me you already heard back from the Fire Prevention magazine editor?"

"Not yet, and I don't expect to for a while. This is about Owen."

"I'm already intrigued. Does he or doesn't he have a girlfriend?"

The question reminded Hallie how long it'd been since she and Paige had spoken. "He doesn't," she said.

"All right. And?"

"We've been spending a fair amount of time together."

"You're dating."

Hallie pictured her friend rubbing her hands together in gleeful approval. "Not in the formal sense, but we are getting to know each other. He comes over and he took me to the hardware store the other day. We talk a lot and do other things."

"Define 'other things.' "

"As much as I love you, Paige, that's a little too per-

sonal. Let's leave it at I want him and he wants me."
Even saying the words made Hallie hungry for him.

"I can hardly believe my ears. This is a huge change for you." Paige lowered her voice. "How's the sex?"

"We're not there yet. Owen doesn't think I'm ready."

"He's not pressuring you?"

"Not at all."

"He sounds like a decent guy," Paige said. "Suddenly I like him a lot."

"Yeah, he's great."

"I sense a 'but.'"

"He's been buried under a project for days now and won't be finished until next weekend. I miss him something awful."

"Really." Paige hesitated a moment as if thinking about that. "You're falling for him."

"I'm not," Hallie assured her. "I don't let myself even think about that. He's told me umpteen times he isn't interested in a serious relationship. My heart is hardly healed from losing Simon and I don't know that I could bear having it broken again."

"That seems wise. God knows, we've both been hurt more than enough. Be careful, okay?

"You're the one who's been encouraging me to try casual sex."

"This doesn't sound casual."

"All I know is, I ache for him." Hallie wanted—no, needed—to make love with him. "These past few days I've done a lot of thinking. Owen doesn't know it yet, but I am ready."

"He's bound to be happy about that. When are you going to tell him?"

"The next time I see him, or I might show him in-

stead. I haven't decided. Either way, he'll be surprised."
Hallie glanced at the clock. "Shoot, I'm due at my parents' soon. I'd better go. I'll talk to you later."

HALLIE WAS a few miles from the Sawyer compound when her cell phone rang. "Libby," her Bluetooth announced.

"Hi," Hallie said.

Her sister murmured something unintelligible. Hallie frowned. "Speak up—I can't hear you."

"I don't dare. I'm in the bathroom, but you never know where Mom might be."

"Ah, you're at the big house. I'll be there in under ten minutes. Whisper it to me then."

"You need to know now. Hang on while I turn on the fan." Hallie heard the whirring sound.

"There," Libby said.

"What's so important it can't wait?"

"Mom and Dad know about Owen and General Hardware."

"We ran into Mom there. Owen took me to buy solar lights for my—"

"About you two kissing in the parking lot."

"What?" Hallie nearly ran off the road. She straightened the wheels and slowed way down. "How did they find out?"

"Two words—Betty Randall."

That explained the woman's sly smile at the auto shop. "We were the only car in the very back row of the parking lot. No one else was around."

"Well, someone saw."

The kiss had blotted out everything else, but now that Hallie thought about it... "There may have been a honking car and a snide comment." She groaned. "What did Mom say?"

"Not much. I think she's saving most of her comments for you."

"I can hardly wait," Hallie muttered. "Thanks for the heads-up."

Some minutes later she entered the house with her shoulders squared.

Her mother didn't even greet her before she started in. "I knew something was going on between you and Owen," she said in a singsong tone. "Your father and I are thrilled for you."

"Hello to you, too, Mom. Don't jump to any conclusions. It was just a kiss."

Slight underexaggeration. That kiss had opened the door to a new phase of Hallie's life—Owen rocking her world. In the very near future she intended to rock his. She managed a careless shrug. "I don't want to talk about it."

"I understand, honey. I won't say another word."

Ha.

Throughout the meal the entire family teased her.

"Owen's a catch," Joe said.

"Like a fish?" Caleb, his eight year-old son, asked.

"In a way," Libby replied. "It's an old-fashioned term for a man or a woman who'd make a good partner, someone you might want to marry." She gave Joe a dirty look. "Guys don't refer to other guys as 'a catch.' "

Brett jumped to his brother's defense. "He's saying Owen is a good guy."

"I'd sure like to meet him." Joe's wife, Noreen, glanced at Libby and Angela. "Wouldn't you?"

Libby grinned. "Do you even have to ask?"

"Too bad, Lib—you're already taken," Chase quipped. "I'd like to get an up-close look at him myself and see what all the fuss is about. I've never met a fire-fighter."

"Owen's a firefighter?" Caleb looked impressed. "I want to meet him, too."

Taking a cue from their oldest cousin, the other kids chimed in with similar comments.

"So would Grandpa and I," Gran said. "Everyone wants to meet your Owen."

Hallie ground her teeth. "He's not mine."

"Why don't you invite him to dinner next Sunday?" her father suggested.

Subject the poor guy to the entire family's scrutiny? "It isn't that kind of relationship," she replied. "I can't handle anything serious."

"Who said anything about serious?"

"That's right," her mother said. "The important thing is, you're finally seeing someone."

"When do we get dessert?" Caleb asked.

Bless him. For a few happy minutes all attention focused on clearing the table and the peach pies Gran had made, Hallie's favorite. Though her mouth watered, she'd had enough of her family. She wanted out of there more than she wanted pie.

"None for me, thanks," she said. "I should get home."

Her mother snorted. "You don't need to watch your weight, honey. I'm sure Owen likes you just as you are."

Hallie narrowed her eyes. "Mom..."

Gran laid a calming hand on Hallie's arm. "Leave her alone, Sandy. You can take yours home with you, Hallie. I'll cut your piece right away."

"Make it enough for two," her mother said with a calculating smile. "In case she's expecting company later."

Ignoring the comment, Hallie stood. "A normal-size piece is fine, Gran. Thanks for dinner, Mom and Dad."

While her grandmother found a paper plate and covered the wedge of pie in plastic wrap, Libby made the "call me" sign with her fingers.

Hallie nodded, took her dessert, and left.

23

After a long weekend spent hunched in front of his keyboard, ironing kinks out of the training program, Owen was sick of the whole thing and glad to be at the station.

He stowed his personal stuff in the tiny room he called home for forty-eight hours every week, then headed toward the kitchen with the breakfast special from Rosemary's and two sack lunches.

He greeted his crewmates, found a seat at the big table, opened his breakfast container and dug in.

"Did you get the solar lighting installed at Hallie's?" Rafe asked, munching his own food.

"Yep—with Hank's and Max's help."

Hank nodded. "Hallie paid us in pizza, beer, and cookies. On our way back to town, Max and I stopped at Field's Sports Bar to grab a pitcher and watch the baseball game. The Seattle Mariners rocked."

"In the end, they did." Rafe launched a conversation about the ninth inning, which had almost spilled into an extra inning. "Did you see that triple play, Owen?"

Owen shook his head. "I didn't catch the game."

"Hallie doesn't like baseball?"

"The subject hasn't come up." He'd been too busy, making her moan and quiver to talk sports.

His crewmates snickered and he gave an amiable shrug.

Hottest week of his life without sex, and he was paying for it. He hadn't been this horny since the early years of high school.

The alarm sounded, and dispatcher Sarah McCone called all paramedics to action. That meant Owen—his month-long paramedic rotation started today.

Abandoning his breakfast, he jumped up.

Moments later, Daniel at the wheel, Owen riding shotgun, and Nate in the back, they sped toward for the first emergency of the day. Owen didn't get a chance to sit down, let alone think, until evening.

As soon as he made up the bed in his temporary room, he toed off his shoes, slid his cell phone from his pocket, and dropped wearily to the mattress. After four days apart, he missed Hallie. He stretched out on the mattress and phoned her.

"Hi," she said, sounding pleased to hear from him.

"Hi. Do you like baseball?"

"Sure. Do you?"

"Yeah."

"Is there a reason you asked?" she said.

"Just wondered."

"Now you know. You sound tired."

"Started my paramedic rotation today and we were busy. Two heart attacks, a broken leg, a drug overdose, and a panic attack. Topped off late this afternoon by a four-hundred-pound male who got stuck in a shower."

"I assume you managed to get him out."

"With a little creative maneuvering and a lot of sweat."

"Sounds challenging."

"This job is never boring, that's for sure. How was your day?"

"Easier than yours. I sketched out two new articles, one featuring local wineries and another about our orchards. I emailed both pitches to an airline magazine that has published my articles before. More often than not, they buy my work. And I set up a tour and interview at Rogue Valley Winery. I'm also waiting for a call back from the PR people at Marks' Orchards."

Owen admired her work ethic. "You don't waste any time."

"I can't afford to. Now that the editor at the magazine knows me, she's usually quick to respond."

"Any word on the firefighters series?"

"Yesterday my best friend, Paige, asked the same thing. I probably won't hear for a while yet. Did you fix whatever glitches your beta testers found?"

"Pretty much. I need a day or two for a comb-through and a final check. I should finish Friday. I'd better—I promised Opal we'd cook dinner for Pearl that night."

"You're a good uncle. Congrats on the project! I've only spoken to Pearl once since she started her new job. How are she and Opal doing?"

"They both seem happy, but at night Pearl's back still bothers her some. Opal likes her teacher and has made lots of new friends."

"That's great. Speaking of dinner, the one at my parents' last night was weird."

"How so?"

"Remember when I ran into Betty Randall at the auto shop and the sly smile she gave me? I found why —she knows about our kiss in the hardware store parking lot."

"How the hell did she find out?"

"I have no idea, but she went straight to my mother and probably everyone else in town. Mom told the rest of our family."

Owen could guess how that had gone over. "What'd they say?"

"They all want to meet you. My dad even suggested I bring you to Sunday dinner."

Did Hallie want more than Owen could give? He tensed. "I don't think that's a good idea."

"Which is why I explained that we don't have that kind of relationship and you wouldn't be joining us."

Still on the same page, then. He relaxed. "Thanks for getting me out of that. If things go as planned with the training program, I'll be in the mood to celebrate Friday night—and I don't mean with Pearl and Opal. After dinner, you and I should go out."

"Or we could be alone together."

Images of Hallie, flushed and aroused, crowded his mind. "I wish I was with you right now."

"Don't or you'll get me all hot and bothered."

A certain part of him stirred to attention. Too bad she wasn't ready to make love. "I'll be over after dinner with a bottle of champagne," he said. "I'll bring a movie, too." To cool them both down. "Do you prefer comedies, dramas, or thrillers?"

"Anything is fine."

"Come on, Hallie, choose a category."

"How about a funny thriller-drama?"

Owen chuckled. "I'll do my best."

TELL OWEN she was ready to make love, or show him —and if so, how? After deliberating for days, she figured out a plan that incorporated both telling and showing.

Friday night finally arrived. Hallie spent an hour bathing in lilac-scented bubble bath and otherwise making herself desirable. She couldn't wait to see the look on his face.

But when he knocked at her door she faltered. Ten minutes ago the red satin-lace teddy and strappy heels had seemed the perfect way to greet him, and yet...

For all her consuming lust, it'd been so long since she'd brought a man to her bed, and never a man she wasn't in love with. Could she go through with this?

Yes. She and Owen would share a wonderful evening together—as long as she didn't fall for him. I won't, she pledged, and mentally secured the lock on her heart. She felt much better, but anxious about the act itself.

Standing on his hind legs, Wilbur scratched at the door and barked. "Down," she ordered before answering. "Hi, Owen." Feeling oddly shy, she stood back and let him in.

His eyes almost popped out of his head. Not about to be ignored, Wilbur clamored for attention, but for once, Owen paid no attention to the animal. "Wow," he said, setting the champagne and DVD aside. "That's some outfit."

Under his heavy-lidded expression her worries fled. "I thought you'd like it."

"Like it? You look amazing—but you're playing with fire."

"Which is exactly what I'm aiming for."

"Are you saying what I think you are?"

She nodded. "I'm ready, Owen."

Desire glowed hot in his eyes. "No wonder you didn't care about the movie."

He reached for her. In her four-inch heels, she stood eye-level to his shoulder. Cupping her bottom, he anchored her to his hips. One demanding and hungry kiss and all felt right with the world.

Wilbur nudged between them and broke the spell. The jitters returned, Hallie's nerves jangling every bit as much as Wilbur's dog tags.

Oblivious, Owen bent to pet the lab. "Hi, buddy. How ya doing?"

The dog calmed down right away and soon trotted off for a nap.

"How was dinner?" she asked.

"Opal and I made a decent casserole. She was so proud, and Pearl was all smiles. Pearl says 'Hi' and she'll phone you soon.

"If I'd known about you, about this... I'd have switched the meal to a different night and come over a lot earlier. Did you just decide today?"

"I made up my mind about a week ago, but I wanted to surprise you."

"Mission accomplished. Too bad I only have one condom on me—the one I keep in my wallet."

"Don't worry—I bought a whole box."

"Excellent." He grinned. A glance at her fidgety fingers sobered him. "Maybe we should wait longer."

"No. I want this. I just... I'm out of practice."

"It's like riding a bike. Once you know how, you never forget." He grasped a lock of her meticulously straightened hair and gave it a playful tug. "We're already good together, so relax."

She nodded. When a few deep breaths failed to help, she chewed the pad of her thumb.

"You're still nervous. Dr. Owen to the rescue." He gestured at the couch. "Sit."

"Not here." She took his hand and led him to the

bedroom, which was about the size of his entry and not half as nice. But the rosy glow of the bedside table lamp and the turned-back covers made the room look cozy and inviting.

"I can't fit anything bigger than a double bed in here," she apologized.

"We'll make it work. Take a seat."

Hallie perched on the edge of the bed. Owen knelt at her feet and removed her shoes. Cupping one foot in his big, warm hands, he began, massaging her toes, her arch, her ankle.

Delicious warmth spread through her, leaving no space for anything else. "That feels amazing," she said.

"Pearl's physical therapist taught me the technique. After her surgery I massaged her feet every day to help lessen the pain."

"Lucky Pearl."

"Time to switch feet."

For a while Hallie stopped talking, too caught up in the pleasure to speak. Soon she was limp as a ragdoll.

Owen sat back on his heels. "You're not nervous anymore."

"My bones feel like melted butter. If you ever decide to retire from the fire department and give up your training program business, you could start a new career as a masseur."

Laughing softly, he nodded toward the pillows. "Scoot back."

The mattress dipped as he joined her on the bed. "I think you need a little more work." He kneaded her calf muscles, then around her knees. "You have great legs."

"You have great hands."

Slowly he worked his way up her thighs. All the

way up. He stoked her most sensitive part through the satin until she was wet and crazed with need.

His burning gaze raked over her. "You're tense again."

"Because I'm going up in flames. Please, do something."

A grin of pure male satisfaction bloomed on his face. "This time when you come I'll be deep inside you. I want you naked—now. Turn around."

He slid the straps from her shoulders, his touch both tender and seductive. Pulled down the zipper in back, brushed her hair aside and planted open-mouth kisses along her exposed skin.

Hallie shivered. Aroused and ready she swiveled her head and looked at him over her shoulder. "I thought you wanted me naked."

"Patience, Hallie."

He removed his shirt and tossed it somewhere. Her satin lace teddy pooled at her waist. From behind, he wrapped his arms around her and cupped her breasts.

Unable to bear any more pleasure without climaxing, she batted him away. Facing him, she stripped the teddy off herself. For all the times he'd pleasured her, he'd never seen her completely nude. Would he like what he saw?

His warm gaze made her feel flawless and desirable.

"You're beautiful—a goddess."

No other man had ever described her that way. She liked it a lot. Emboldened by his words she pushed him onto his back. "No fair—I'm the only naked person here. Those jeans must go." She reached for his fly and started to lower the zipper.

Owen stopped her. "No, Hallie. I'm too close to the edge."

"You take them off, then, and I'll open the box of condoms."

By the time she handed him a condom he was naked. Gloriously aroused, he sheathed himself. Hallie waited for him with open arms.

He levered himself above her. "I'll try to go slow."

His arms shook with the effort of holding back. Hallie raised up to meet him. "I don't want slow."

In one deep thrust he entered her. A moan slid from her throat.

He froze. "Too fast?"

"Not fast enough. Hurry."

Desperate for release, she gripped his hips with her thighs and urged him on. As her muscles began to contract in a shuddering climax, he growled and came with her.

Sometime later, when her heartbeat slowed and the world righted itself, she opened her eyes. Propped on his elbow, he wore the look of a satisfied man. "Told you you wouldn't forget how."

Hallie beamed. "Thanks to you."

"You're good?"

"I'm fabulous."

His satisfied grin made her knees go weak. He kissed her shoulder, flipped the lamp off, and lay down beside her.

Drowsy and sated she curled against his side. For the first time in ages she felt truly content. Owen in her bed, his masculine scent marking her body and the warm heaviness of his hand on her hip, was heaven.

As she hovered on the verge of sleep her mind ran free. She imagined sharing a bed with him every night and a lifetime of nights like this. The wayward thought snapped her eyes open. Wide awake now, she stared into the darkness.

There is no future with Owen.

And that was okay. After all, she didn't love him. Hallie willed herself to believe that. Her peace of mind and the safety of her heart depended on it.

24

Best. Sex. Ever. Feeling great, Owen anchored Hallie nice and close. As soon as he recovered he'd go in for a repeat.

Later in the week she could stay at his place, or he'd come back here. Anywhere was fine, as long as he could be with her.

Slow down. Too much, too soon. He didn't want anything deep, couldn't handle that kind of commitment. Which made him lousy relationship material. Good thing she understood.

But man, he wanted her.

He drifted off for a while, then woke in the middle of an erotic dream, fully erect and spooned around her. She smelled so good, felt soft, and sexy. From behind, he teased her nipples and nuzzled the sensitive crook of her shoulder.

Gasping, she wriggled her sweet behind against his hard-on. Things heated up fast. He was fumbling in the dark with a condom when her cell phone rang.

"Who would call at this hour?" The covers rustled as she reached for her phone on the bedside table.

"Wrong number or prank call?" Owen guessed.

"It's Libby—my sister. A call this late can't be good." She flipped on the lamp.

Owen blinked in the light. Hallie's sharp intake of breath underlined her words. "ER," she said. "Got it. I'll be right there."

Pale as the bed sheet, she disconnected. "My father fainted. He's in the ER at Guff's Lake General."

"What else did your sister say?"

"They don't know what's wrong, but they think he may have a concussion. Apparently he bled quite a bit."

"That happens with scalp wounds." Owen swung his legs over the bed and retrieved his phone. "If they called 911, someone at the station picked him up. They'll be able to fill me in."

"My dad wouldn't let them call anyone. My brother Joe took him. I need to get to the ER right away."

Clutching the lightweight blanket Hallie scrambled up. She snatched clothes from the dresser, rushed from the bedroom into the bathroom, and shut the door behind her.

Owen dressed quickly. "You're in no shape to drive," he commented when she blew back into the bedroom and dropped the blanket on the bed. "I'll take you."

She gave a terse nod. "Let's go."

~

THE NIGHT HAD GROWN COOL, but not uncomfortably so, especially with the Jaguar's top up. All the same, Hallie was cold. She rubbed at her arms, but couldn't seem to get warm.

Owen turned on the heat.

"Thanks." She swallowed hard. "What if my dad had a heart attack?"

"Did your sister mention chest pains or numbness?"

"No, but you don't know my father. He tends to hide his aches and pains." Feeling as if she might throw up, she lowered the window and inhaled the night air.

"Working yourself up this way won't help." Owen caught hold of her hand and wrapped his warm fingers around her icy ones. "It could be something minor."

His calm manner reassured her for a little while, but as he neared the hospital she shuddered. "I hate hospitals. Especially Rogue Valley General."

"FYI, this is an excellent facility—and the only one within fifty miles. Patients here receive top-notch care. Trust me, your dad is in good hands."

"I still hate it." Hallie pulled her hand from his and hugged her waist. "This is where they brought me when I miscarried."

"That must've been rough. I remember when a friend of Colleen's miscarried. She couldn't talk about it without collapsing in tears. Her grief was every bit as painful as if she'd lost a newborn baby. All we could do was offer support and listen when she wanted to talk."

He understood. Not everyone did. "What happened to her?" Hallie asked.

"Over the years we lost touch, but I hear she has a little boy."

"That's wonderful, and very brave of her." Hallie bit her lip, then admitted what she'd never shared with anyone, even Paige. "I could never risk another miscarriage."

Owen nodded. "Your doctor warned you against another pregnancy."

"Nothing like that. I'm able to have children, but I can't imagine living through that kind of loss a second time."

"Who says you will?"

"No one, but it could happen."

He turned into the hospital parking lot and found a space near the ER. Before he set the brake Hallie was out the door, racing toward the entrance.

Catching up to her, he grasped her hand again and laced their fingers together. It meant a lot that he cared.

At this hour the ER was quiet and would have been empty if not for her siblings and grandparents seated in the waiting area. Only the kids and Noreen and Angie, who'd stayed behind with them, were missing. Although Hallie didn't see her mother.

She pulled away from Owen and made a beeline for the group. "How's Dad? Where's Mom?"

"We just learned that he has a mild concussion," Libby said. "The ER doctor recommended other tests, which he's getting now. Mom's with him."

That sounded scary. "Did you say concussion and tests?" Hallie asked.

"Mild concussion," Libby repeated. "The tests are just to be on the safe side. We're waiting now for the results." She slanted her head at Owen. "You're Owen Ayers—I recognize you from the calendar. I'm Hallie's sister, Libby."

"The one who called. Nice to meet you." Owen shook her hand.

The rest of the family stood and crowded around him, with more introductions and hand shaking.

As upset and distracted as Hallie was about her father, she didn't miss the curious looks. She couldn't worry about that now. "What exactly happened to Dad?"

Brett, who'd started a great-to-see-you-even-if-the-timing-sucks conversation with Owen, broke off to explain. "He's had a bad case of the runs, probably from something he ate. Tonight he passed out on the toilet. The doctor mentioned something about an overstimulated nerve."

Owen nodded. "The vaso vagal syncope—or vagus nerve for short."

"That's the one. He managed to get up off the bathroom floor, but he passed out again. On the way down he hit the counter—with his head."

Hallie felt sick all over again. "How long do we have to wait for the test results?"

"No one said, but we know that his vital signs are good and he isn't out of it or confused."

Owen put his arm around her. Hallie welcomed his solid, steady presence.

"Passing out on the toilet is fairly common," he said. "It happens when the vagus nerve becomes irritated. That can cause a drop in the heart rate, which leads to a drop in blood pressure and passing out. If the person tries to get up too soon, they risk passing out again—like your dad did. If someone had called 911 when this happened, the paramedics on duty would have eased your fears right away."

"Our father is a stubborn man," Joe said. "He didn't even want to come to the ER. Brett and I had to strong-arm him into the car."

"Sometimes that man is too hard-headed for his own good." Gran elbowed Grandpa. "He got that from you."

After what seemed forever, Hallie's parents entered the waiting room.

"All the tests are normal," her mother said.

Relief all around.

Her dad looked sheepish. "Sorry to bring you out so late, kiddo."

"You look like you just rolled out of bed," her mom commented.

Hallie knew she was blushing. "I rushed over as soon as Libby called. I didn't bother to fix myself up."

"Ah." Her mother eyed Owen. "Hello again. This is my husband, Jim."

"So you're the firefighter I've been hearing about," Hallie's father said as they shook hands. "A shame we had to meet under these circumstances."

"I'm glad you're okay. It's a good idea to contact your doctor in the morning."

Naturally he waved that suggestion away. "No need —I'm fine. Or I will be, once I get some sleep."

"Don't count on that tonight," Hallie's mother warned. "I'll be waking you every few hours."

"I'll call you tomorrow, Dad," Hallie promised.

"If you must." Her parents linked arms and started toward the elevators.

The rest of the family followed en masse. Hallie held Owen back. "Let's wait until they're gone," she said in a voice too soft for the others to hear.

Her stomach growled and Owen grinned. "I'm running on empty, too. I happen to know where to find the nearest vending machine. How about a chocolate bar?"

"Yes, please."

Five minutes later the family had disappeared and so had Hallie's candy. She licked her lips. "That was just what I needed. Now we can go."

25

It was after midnight when Owen and Hallie piled into the Jag. After a long few hours at the ER, he was ready to call it a night. Hallie was quiet, probably just as exhausted.

"How are you doing?" he asked as he pulled onto the road.

"Relieved about my dad, of course. I didn't realize how tired I am until now."

Having been there himself countless times, Owen could identify. "What you're feeling is a classic after-effect following an adrenaline surge."

She drew her eyebrows together. "I'm not sure I had one."

"Trust me, you did. Think back to your mental and physical reactions after Libby called. Your focus grew razor-sharp, your heart raced, and your breathing quickened—all indicators of an adrenaline surge. You didn't let down until you learned your dad was okay. When the surge fades, what's left is fatigue."

"I had no idea. I've never met a man who knows so much about so many things. Your IQ must be off the charts."

So people had told him. He gave a modest shrug. "I

know about adrenaline surges because I experience them with almost every call. All firefighters do."

"That makes sense. Shoot, I wish I'd known before I sent off the article. A detail like that would have added a degree of richness to the piece."

"Richness—there's something I never considered. You're pretty sharp yourself."

"Thanks. I can write about adrenaline surges in the next fire department profile—if the editor approves my series. I expect to hear any day now. Cross your fingers."

"They're crossed." Owen hoped she got what she wanted.

For several miles they rode in comfortable silence. Hallie had turned toward the window and didn't move much. Owen figured she'd fallen asleep.

Then she pivoted toward him. "I never considered you'd be stuck meeting so many of my family members tonight."

"They aren't so bad."

"My brothers and sister are great and my grandparents are okay, but there are times when my parents drive me crazy. Do I really look like I just rolled out of bed?"

"You look fine. Anyway that's exactly what we did —got up, got dressed, and came straight to the ER."

"You're missing the point. They know you and I were together." She put her head in her hands and groaned. "Family dinner this Sunday is sure to be even worse than last week's."

It couldn't be that bad. Owen fought a grin. "Would you rather I'd stayed home tonight?"

"Are you kidding? I don't regret one second of what we did."

In the dim light from the street lamps her eyes shone with a soft, sweet intensity that worried him.

"You're an amazing lover," she added, touching her tongue to her upper lip, those eyes now heavy-lidded and seductive again.

He'd mistaken passion for deeper feelings. Relief and his rising desire banished his concerns. He wanted to pull the car over and make love with her. But the Jag was no place for that. Also, she'd been through a lot this evening and they were both beat.

No more loving tonight.

Awhile later he pulled up Hallie's driveway.

"You were wonderful tonight," she said as he walked her to the door.

"Which part?" he teased.

"All of it." She pulled him down for a good-night kiss.

"I need to see you again soon," he growled, his forehead against hers.

"I like the sound of that, Mr. Ayers. Call me."

"Count on it."

~

"HELLUVA WAY TO START A MONDAY," Owen commented from the shotgun seat as he and his paramedic crewmates headed toward to the station from Rogue Valley General. "Swallowing half a bottle of laxatives to lose weight—what was that woman thinking?"

Nate, the designated aid-car driver, shook his head. "Who knows. As dehydrated as she was, she's lucky we rushed her to the ER. Must be a full moon."

In back, Daniel snorted. "Don't need a calendar to know that."

"Hallie's dad ended up at the ER the other night," Owen said.

The other men made sympathetic sounds. "He okay?" Nate asked.

Owen nodded. "Vaso vagal syncope and a mild concussion. Freaked the whole family out."

"Which shift picked him up?"

"He refused to call for help. Hallie's brothers took him."

"You don't mess around with a concussion," Daniel muttered.

"You know how bull-headed some people are. He seems like a stand-up guy, though."

"So you met Hallie's father." Nate whistled. "You move fast. Not that I blame you, you lucky dog. Hallie's something special."

Owen agreed. Saturday night he'd invited her to his place to join him, Pearl, and Opal for dinner and a movie. After his niece and sister turned in, Hallie had stuck around, staying until near dawn for another fantastic night. He felt incredibly lucky.

But Nate had it all wrong.

"It's not what you think," he said. "I was with her when she got the call that her dad was in the ER. She was pretty upset so I drove her to the hospital. That's where I met her dad and some of the other family members."

Owen's bud frowned. "I figured you were in a relationship."

"Yeah, but nothing heavy."

"Friends with benefits—I get it."

"I tried that once." Daniel gave his head a dire shake. "Things were good until she decided she wanted a different type of benefit—an engagement ring and a wedding."

"That won't happen with Hallie and me," Owen assured him. "She knows the score."

"That's exactly what I thought. Be careful, man."

Occupied with thoughts of seeing Hallie again after his double shift ended, Owen barely heard the warning. Wednesday couldn't come soon enough.

26

Yawning, Hallie fed Wilber just after dawn Wednesday morning. Then she sat down with a cup of coffee to wake up. By the time he licked the last morsel of food from his bowl she was alert enough to check email.

John Bodine had sent her the galleys of her article to look over and correct if needed—with a forty-eight-hour turnaround.

She also found good news from the editor at the airline magazine. The woman requested both the winery and orchard articles. Hooray!

On the downside, she wanted them in two weeks. With no time to waste, Hallie e-signed the attached contracts and sent them back. She would take care of the galleys first, then tackle the winery piece.

She'd barely started on the galleys when Owen texted. Meet me at Rosemary's for breakfast.

Thoughts of work fled. Hallie smiled with such elation that every cell in her body followed suit.

Not because she loved him—she didn't and wouldn't, period—but because she hadn't seen him in three long days, since she'd tiptoed out his front door early Sunday morning after a wonderful night together. She was thrilled about seeing him again, and who could blame her?

Eager to join him, she texted back. What time?

8:15.

See you then. Got the galleys for the fire department article today, and good news from the airline magazine. They want both the winery and the orchard articles!!!

Atta girl.

Thanks to rush hour and the first heavy rain of the fall, traffic was slower than usual. Hallie pulled up at the breakfast café a few minutes late.

Through the front window she spotted Owen at a large table with Hank, Max, Rafe, his girlfriend Jillian, Adam, and Samantha. A whole lot of handsome in one place.

But Owen was the one who stole Hallie's breath. And he was all hers.

For the moment, she reminded herself. At times she couldn't help but wonder what she'd do when they tired of each other. Her heart squeezed. Why am I stressing about this now, when things are going so well?

Dismissing her worries and firmly in control of her emotions she stepped through the door. The delicious aromas wafting through the café made her mouth water. Owen threw back his head and laughed at something. Hallie had no idea what was funny but she smiled anyway.

As if sensing her presence, he looked straight at her with an approving gaze at her fitted blouse and flouncy skirt. When she reached the table he tugged her onto the empty seat beside him and kissed her— right there in public.

She started to get all hot and bothered. Had they

been alone, she would have climbed onto his lap and seduced him.

"Hallie just sold two articles to an airline magazine," he announced to the others at the table, his arm around her. After congratulations all around, he opened a menu and shared it with her. "What would you like?"

Under the table, he ran his hand up her inner thigh, all the way to her panties. She bit back a moan. In a voice for her ears only he added, "We could head to my place for our own private meal."

Although seriously tempted, she pushed his hand away. "Mr. One-Track Mind. I need actual food."

"Yeah, me too. We'll go to my place after breakfast —for dessert."

"Mm, that sounds good."

Even though Pearl and Opal had turned in early the other night, giving her and Owen plenty of privacy, Hallie had felt inhibited.

Today they would have the house to themselves.

She could hardly wait.

RELAXED IN OWEN'S giant soaker tub and cradled from behind in his arms, Hallie sighed in contentment. "I've never had sex in a bathtub."

"I've been fantasizing about us together in here since the other night." He nuzzled the crook of her neck, sending fresh pleasure through her. "The temperature's cooling down. Why don't I add more hot water and turn on the jets?"

"No thanks. I'm starting to turn into a prune. I need to get out. "

"Stay put."

He stood and stepped from the tub. Water dripped from his beautiful body onto the throw rug. Unself-conscious, he dried off and secured a towel around his hips.

He brought Hallie a fresh, oversize towel. As soon as she stood, he wrapped her in it and picked her up as if she weighed nothing.

"Better?" he asked, setting her down.

"About as good as it can get."

"Damn straight. I sure missed you."

"It's only been a few days."

"Missed you anyway." He smiled tenderly and kissed the tip of her nose.

With that sweet gesture of affection something inside her shifted. Her heart expanded with the most profound warmth and sweetness imaginable, dissolving her self-control and flooding her with the feelings she'd fought and denied for weeks.

Love.

She loved Owen, and no use lying to herself about it anymore.

Nothing good would come of this. He didn't want her love any more than she wanted to love him. Regardless, it was happening. Had happened.

Panicky and frightened, she ducked her head against his probing gaze.

"Hey." He tipped up her chin. "Something wrong?"

Everything! She made herself meet his eyes. "It's after twelve, later than I realized. I need to work on the galleys and the wine and orchard articles. And poor Wilbur has been inside for hours."

"He's fine." Warm hands cupped her shoulders. "Put off work until later and spend the afternoon with me."

"I can't, Owen." Securing her towel with one hand,

she scooped her clothes from the floor with the other. "I'll dress in the powder room."

"What for?"

She forced a teasing smile. "You're too distracting."

Anxious to leave the house, she hurried into her clothes. She ran her brush quickly through her wet hair, which was already starting to curl, and pulled it into a ponytail.

When she entered the living room Owen was waiting.

"I don't think you've ever dressed this fast," he commented. "Not even when your dad was in the ER."

"A girl's gotta do what she must."

He walked her to the door and kissed her. "Call you later."

Hallie nodded. And prayed she could shut her feelings down before Owen moved on and her heart broke in two.

27

Not long after Hallie left Owen's she realized she'd left her hairbrush in his powder room. Her favorite brush, too. It wasn't the first time she'd forgotten something when she was with him. Her camera, her brush...

But this morning's staggering brain lapse took the blue-ribbon prize. She'd let go of her self-control and released the lock on her heart. Now she was in a world of trouble.

She needed Paige. Too shaken to use the Bluetooth in her car, she wheeled into a convenience store parking lot, braked to a stop, and texted her friend. SOS. Code for I need you!

Instantly Paige replied. Today, 4:00. Coffee Shack.

Their usual meeting place, and about halfway between Hallie's cottage and the factory where her friend worked.

Hallie blew out a relieved breath. Help was on the way—even if she did have to wait several more hours.

THE COFFEE SHACK was located mere miles from Guff's Lake, which lay nestled in the foothills of the Siskiyou Mountains. Thanks to the excellent coffee and spectacular view of the town's namesake the Shack was always packed.

Today was no exception. After some searching, Hallie spotted Paige at a small table in the corner.

Hallie waved, then pointed at the counter, where she stopped to order a decaf and two brownies. Within minutes she set her purchases on the table.

"So good to see you," she said, greeting Paige with a much-needed hug. "FYI, I haven't heard anything about the Fire Prevention magazine series, although I did sell two articles to an airline magazine."

"Congrats, but I don't think you SOS'd me just to tell me that." Paige eyed the brownies and gave a knowing nod. "Let me guess—something happened with Owen."

"Yes." As noisy as the café was, eavesdroppers could be anywhere. Hallie leaned forward and lowered her voice. "When you and I last talked I was planning to surprise him. I did, and now everything's changed."

She ate a big bite of brownie. So did Paige, who refrained from commenting—her way of letting Hallie share at her own pace.

"It's been wonderful," Hallie said. "And it keeps getting better and better. Or did until this morning, when I realized my feelings are bigger than just sex. I think I love him. No, I do love him."

Unable to eat one more bite of brownie, she pushed the plate aside. "Tell me I've confused the feel of his arms around me with love, that it happened too fast to be real."

She wanted so much for Paige to reassure her. Instead, her friend did the opposite. "If you remember, the same thing happened with me. After one date with Milo, I fell hard."

Hallie groaned. "You're not helping. Milo's feelings echoed yours. Owen doesn't want that kind of relationship. How do I stop loving him?"

"Oh, sweetie. I don't think you can fight your heart."

Hallie knew that but she'd hoped for a suggestion or two. A sigh of pure misery slipped out.

"Maybe this isn't as one-sided as you think. What if Owen's feelings for you are equally strong and he's just as wary?"

Hallie remembered his affection and warmth in the afterglow this morning. Of course he'd been tender—the sex had been amazing. "He feels things for me, all right—physical desire. Yes, he likes me, but that's as far as it goes. He went through a bad divorce."

"You've been through a lot worse than that, yet here you are, head over heels."

"And totally freaked out."

"You don't have to marry the man or tell him you love him. Unless you already have."

"Are you kidding? He doesn't have a clue."

"Then there's no reason to panic."

"I wish you'd explain that to my brain, because I'm petrified. Look." Hallie held out her fingers. Thanks to a bad case of nerves, she'd chewed her nails almost to the quick. "I am sure of one thing—a relationship based on sex isn't working for me. Don't get me wrong, I love being with him and wish what we share could grow and deepen, but I'm not naive. Someday he'll leave and I'll be left to pick up the pieces of my heart."

Resting her head in her hands, she stared morosely at the scarred surface of the table. "I'd rather be celibate than in love."

"Wow."

"Yeah." In a sudden change of mind, Hallie polished off the brownie.

"At least you know what you want."

"You mean what I don't want. I guess that's that." Hallie brushed her hands together. "Good-bye, Owen."

Her friend's eyes widened. "You're going to break up with him? Are you sure you want to?"

"I can't just sit around and wait for the ax to fall."

"Okay. What are you going to tell him?"

Hallie hadn't given that much thought. "It's over."

"Of course, but you need to lead into the subject."

That did seem fair. The mere thought of that conversation filled Hallie with dread. She grimaced. "I can't tell him I love him. What exactly should I say?"

"For starters, the same thing you told me—that you're not cut out for a sex-only relationship."

"But then he might guess my real feelings. He's super smart."

"You're breaking up with him, Hallie. What does it matter if he figures out the truth?"

"It just does. A matter of pride, I guess. I convinced him I wasn't any more susceptible to falling in love than he is. I tried to convince myself, too. That sure worked well." Hallie laughed without humor.

"Like I said, the heart has a mind of its own."

"There's something else, too." Hallie swallowed hard and confessed an underlying fear no one else would understand. "I'm afraid I'll forget Simon."

"Is that what this is about?"

"No, but since I met Owen...it's been on my mind."

"You'll never forget him."

"Every day he slips further away from me." Hallie

could barely remember the sound of her late fiancé's voice. "I used to go days without thinking about him. Since Owen, it's been weeks." Her eyes filled. "How do I handle the guilt?"

"When I was freaking over my feelings for Milo, you assured me Jacob wouldn't want me to waste my life pining over him. It's my turn to say the same to you." Paige gave a watery smile. "No matter how much I love Milo, Jacob will always be right here." She tapped the place above her heart. "That's where you'll find Simon."

Hallie sniffled. "I think I knew that, but I needed to hear it." She rifled through her purse for a packet of tissues, then handed one to Paige. They both paused to dab their eyes.

"What are you going to do about Owen?" Paige asked.

"What you said—have a talk that ends with our breakup."

Page nodded, then checked her watch. "I should get back to the factory and tie up a few ends before I go home. Call or text anytime."

"I will. I never got a chance to hear about you," Hallie said as they exited the café.

"I'm not pregnant yet, but it's only been six weeks."

Was that all? So much had changed in Hallie's life, it seemed longer. "It's bound to happen soon," she said. "Thanks for meeting me in the middle of a work day. I don't know what I'd do without you."

"Same here."

After exchanging hugs, they parted and went their separate ways.

28

"Hallie left her brush in the powder room," Pearl commented when she arrived home from work Wednesday. Opal was in her room, playing. "You didn't mention she was here today."

"So?" Owen shrugged. He didn't understand his sister's dirty look. "What's the big deal? We're talking about a hairbrush. I'll get it back to her tonight."

"I don't care about the brush, but I do care about you and Hallie. What are you doing, Owen?"

"Enjoying each other—not that it's any of your business."

"It is if my friend gets hurt."

"She won't. We have an understanding."

"Are you sure about that?"

Pretty much. Hallie seemed as happy with their relationship as he was. True, the tension he'd sensed before she'd taken off earlier had seemed out of place. At the time he'd assumed she was uptight about getting her work done, but... Uneasy, he squinted at his sister. "Why, did she say something I need to know?"

"She didn't have to. I saw the way she looked at you when she came over Saturday night."

Owen had noticed, too. Before he and Hallie had made love, the same soft, yet heated expression had given him pause. Now he understood that look was all about the sex neither of them could get enough of. He snorted. "You don't know what you're talking about. Butt out."

Despite his words and silent self-assurances, his sister's concerns ate at him. Was Hallie stressed over her writing projects or something else?

He needed to find out.

ON THE DRIVE back to the cottage Hallie mulled over what to say to Owen when she ended the relationship. The thought of never seeing him again made her heart ache, but dragging things out would only hurt worse later.

She'd rather have a root canal than the dreaded conversation, but Paige was right. Talking about it was the decent thing to do. If only she knew the right words. Something about a sex-only relationship not working for her, but what else?

Until she figured out something that sounded plausible—other than I love you, which she would never admit to him—breaking up would have to wait.

Granting herself a short reprieve eased her anxiety. Maybe she'd come up with a believable reason while her mind was occupied elsewhere. For the remainder of the trip home she turned her thoughts to other pressing needs—the winery article and what to fix for dinner. By the time she parked in the carport she felt better, in control.

Wilbur demanded attention and got it. "I'm glad to see you, too." Hallie opened the back door and shooed him out. "Go do your potty thing. I need to write, but I'll leave this open. When you want in, woof at the screen door."

Hunched over her laptop at the kitchen table, she got down to work.

Wilbur didn't stay out long. Content, he curled up near her feet and napped.

After several solid hours at the keyboard, with short breaks to make herself a grilled cheese sandwich and feed Wilbur, Hallie finished a very rough draft of her winery article and congratulated herself for not thinking about Owen since sitting down.

Well, maybe once or twice.

"I'm a professional writer—why can't I figure out what to say to him?" she lamented.

Wilbur cocked his head and gave her a sorrowful expression as if he sympathized.

"You're right—the best thing for me is to keep busy and trust that the words will come to me. But I can only focus so long before I reach my limit and brain overload sets in. I'm done for today. I may as well find something on the tube."

Hallie flopped on the couch and tuned to a sitcom she liked. The show always made her smile, but tonight nothing was funny. Or maybe the problem lay with her.

After muting the sound she frowned at what was left of her wretched nails and mourned the loss of her relationship with Owen. She would miss him so much.

Suddenly Wilbur cocked his ears. Tail wagging, he raced to the front door. A breath later Hallie heard the knock she knew so well.

Owen was here.

Her heart leapt, and not in a good way. Forget waiting until she composed an explanation. Ready or not, it was time to end the relationship.

29

"Hi," Owen said when Hallie answered the door.

She didn't smile, which could mean she was distracted by her work—or not. Unsure what to expect he wiped his feet on the mat and held out her hairbrush. "You left this at my place."

"Thanks." Still solemn as a judge. "I didn't expect to see you tonight."

After greeting Wilbur, Owen straightened. "If you're writing, I'll leave." He glanced past her and noted the tube was on. "Looks as if you're not. That sitcom is one of my favorites. Gonna let me in?"

"It's not very funny tonight." With wooden movements she opened the door all the way.

"You're as uptight as you were when you left my place." He considered massaging her shoulders but decided against it. "What's wrong?"

Her eyes widened, reminding him of a deer caught in someone's headlights. "How did you guess?"

"You don't tense up and stay that way unless something's bothering you. I'm no mind reader. If this is about me, I need to know."

With a resigned sigh she shut the TV off. "Please, sit down," she said, indicating the couch.

Instead of joining him, she took a chair. With grave misgivings he eyed her and waited.

"I..." After hesitating, she muttered something that sounded like, "Spit it out, Hallie," then cleared her throat. "I thought I could handle a sex-only relationship, but I can't. I'm not wired that way."

"We had several conversations about this. Even when I thought we should wait, you pushed for it. That first time you seduced me. You loved every second of what we did. What we do."

She bit her lip and nodded.

"Sex isn't the only thing we have together," he added in the heavy silence.

"You know what I mean."

"What I know is we're good together, both in and out of bed. Sure, we were all about sex this morning, and you rode me in the soaker tub and moaned my name like you couldn't get enough. What changed since then?"

Her cheeks flushed. "I didn't realize until... Oh, never mind." She glanced at her tightly clasped hands.

And he knew. She wanted more from him. Both Nate and Pearl had warned him. Hell, he'd figured that out himself the night she'd cried, and had been reminded more than once since. Each time he'd wanted her so bad he'd ignored the signs and turned a blind eye.

What a selfish bastard he was. He scrubbed the back of his neck. "You don't want a commitment from me, Hallie. I'm a bad bet. Look at my track record."

"I don't have any expectations. I never did. And FYI, I think you're a great guy."

There it was again, the fierce, sweet warmth he

associated with passion alone when he knew better. This time he recognized her emotions for what they were—passion and much more. She had deep feelings for him, way deeper than he'd guessed.

He couldn't do them justice, not in the way she deserved. His heart contracted in his chest. At a loss, he spread his hands. "I don't know what to say, Hallie. I need time to process this."

She squeezed her eyes shut as if it hurt to look at him. "Just go home, Owen. Let yourself out."

For now, that seemed best. "All right. We'll talk soon."

"There's no reason to—it's over."

SITTING on the living room floor with Wilbur at her side, Hallie gulped back a sob and called Paige. "Owen and I just broke up."

"That was fast. I guess you needed to do it right away."

"Yes, and I wasn't ready. It hurts so much, Paige." Hallie was crying outright now. "I feel like I'm dying inside."

"Oh, sweetie. Give me a minute to change out of my PJs and I'll come over."

"Don't bother. It's a long drive and you have to work tomorrow. I just... I need to tell you what happened."

"Please do."

"I was still grappling with the right way to tell him when he stopped by unannounced. I started with what you and I discussed, that I realized I'm not built for a sex-only relationship. The look on his face..."

"Was he angry?"

"More like surprised and confused." Hallie pictured the dawning awareness on his face and swallowed. "I never went near the 'L' word but he read me like an open book. Told you he's smart."

"How did he take it?"

"He felt bad, but it's not his fault I fell in love with him. Then he said he needed to process it. He would have stayed for a while, but I didn't want him to see me break down. I asked him to leave. He accepted that and promised we'd talk soon, and I..." A sob choked off the rest. Pulling herself together, she finished. "I told him not to bother because it was over."

Paige murmured in sympathy. "You don't know that. You caught the man off-guard. Of course he needs time to process."

"I doubt that will make a shred of difference." Hallie blew her nose.

"Maybe, but think about this. He could have cut and run and never looked back, but instead he left the door open for an honest conversation."

"By saying I shouldn't want a commitment from him? That's not my definition of leaving the door open. Neither is 'We'll talk soon.' I don't expect to hear from him. It really is over."

"Don't be too hasty."

Even though Paige couldn't see her, Hallie rolled her eyes.

"Call me back if you need to—tonight or anytime," her friend added.

They disconnected. Emotionally drained, Hallie crawled into bed and curled up into a ball. Paige's advice echoed in her mind, and she couldn't help but hope that once Owen considered the impact of losing what they shared, he'd want a real relationship.

30

After a bad night Owen was tired and out of sorts. In no mood to deal with questions from his sister, he stayed in bed until she and Opal left for the day. Then restless and pissed off at himself for letting things go too far with Hallie, he shoveled down a bowl of cereal, dressed in workout clothes, and headed for Upton's, the gym favored by him and the rest of the crew when off-duty.

At eight a.m. on a Thursday the racquetball and handball courts stood empty. Wanting to burn through his anger, he pulled on protective eyewear and gloves and entered a handball court.

He'd barely started thwacking the ball against the wall before Hank poked his head in. "What are you doing here so early?"

"Needed the workout," Owen replied. "You're usually out running."

"Sometimes a guy needs to switch up. Also, it's supposed to rain hard this morning. How about a game?"

"Why not?"

As soon as his crewmate put on eyewear and gloves,

Owen executed a furious serve. The ball slammed against the wall and whipped toward Hank. Only quick reflexes saved him. When the same thing happened again, he scowled. "You trying to crack my head open?"

"Nope." Owen returned Hank's serve so hard, his palm stung.

Hank let the ball bounce, then caught it. "What the hell is wrong with you?"

Panting from exertion, Owen sucked in air. "Hallie and I broke up last night."

"No way."

"I don't like it either, but she's in love with me." Owen wiped his sweaty forehead with his shirt.

"You just figured that out?"

"You say it as if you knew."

Hank shrugged. "It's been obvious for a while."

"Not to me." Bull. Owen no longer believed that one. Feeling lower than a cockroach, he kicked at the gym floor. "Are we going to finish this game or not?"

Hank served and the action resumed. Two games later they were both breathing hard and dripping sweat.

"You trounced me good," Hank said. "Maybe you'll make it through the rest of the day in a better frame of mind."

At the moment, Owen felt halfway decent, but that could change. "Time will tell."

After showering and dressing he and his bud ambled toward the parking lot. Heavy clouds filled the sky. In the distance, thunder rumbled. "You're right about the weather," he said. "Any second now it's gonna pour."

They upped their pace to reach their cars before the rain started.

"You care about Hallie, right?" Hank asked on the way.

"Yeah. What's your point?"

"I'm no expert on women, but if it were me I'd try to get back together."

Owen didn't even stop to think about that. "I'm no good at long-term relationships. Look how I mucked up my marriage. Hallie can do better than a guy like me."

Although the thought of her with another man made him want to punch something.

Hank's brow furrowed. "I thought Colleen asked you for the divorce."

"Right, but I was as much to blame for what happened as her."

"If you were both at fault maybe you never belonged together in the first place."

"How do you figure that?" Owen asked.

"Otherwise you'd have worked out your problems."

Not true. God knew, Owen had tried. So had Colleen—at least at first. They'd failed.

End of story.

LATELY HALLIE HAD BEEN WAKING up before Wilbur. She wasn't sleeping so well and hadn't been since she'd last seen Owen. Writing, hanging out with Paige, Libby, and other friends, and otherwise keeping busy helped. But nothing eased the constant ache in her heart.

As she tied the sash of her robe and toed into her slippers she rehashed Owen's parting words for the umpteenth time. He needed to process what had happened and they'd talk soon. Paige had agreed with him and urged Hallie to wait for whatever unfolded.

Despite knowing better Hallie had foolishly clung to the hope that maybe, just maybe Paige was onto something, that Owen would realize he wanted a future together. But after nine days of his silence Hallie knew better. She'd been right in the first place—their short-lived relationship was over.

"Breaking up was the right choice for me," she assured herself and Wilbur—again— while he gobbled his breakfast. "But I miss him so much."

The dog barely glanced up from his food.

"I know you're tired of being at my pity party, but I have to talk to someone. Paige and Libby are as sick of hearing about my problems as you, and I'm not about to cry to Pearl." Owen's sister knew they'd stopped seeing each other but not the specifics. "I'll get over him, I promise."

Having licked his bowl clean, Wilbur moved to the door and woofed.

"Some friend you are." Hallie let him out, then let him in again. Not ready to shower and dress or settle down to work—heck, this was Saturday and she was sleepy—she sat down with a fresh cup of coffee and checked email.

Another message from John Bodine at Fire Prevention magazine. Almost a week ago, he'd approved the corrected galleys for her Guff's Lake article. Now the November issue had been printed, and several copies had been mailed to her. Even better, he gave her the green light for the rest of the series.

Three more articles! Wide awake now and elated, she read through the e-contract, signed and sent it back, with a note to send one of her copies to the Guff's Lake Fire Department. She itched to text Owen the good news but he wouldn't want to hear from her. She texted Libby, Paige, and her mother instead.

Next she pulled up the three fire departments at the top of her list. First up, Montrose City, Colorado, which was southwest of Denver. After checking the cost of plane fare she decided to fly to Denver, then rent a car for the last two hundred sixty-five miles of the trip. The drive would take hours but was less expensive than the price of a connecting flight. If it snowed in Colorado—after all, it was October—she'd take a bus from Denver.

Staring into space, she mooned over Owen. She was wondering how she would ever survive the gaping emptiness that now saturated her life when she caught herself.

Put a lid on it, Hallie!

With a lovely, new contract to fulfill she couldn't afford to mope around. The orchard and winery articles were due next week. She needed to polish both right away and send them off—after she scheduled a date to visit the Montrose City Fire Department. Sooner rather than later. She really needed to get away.

With any luck the captain would let her shadow one of the firefighters there. Eager to get started, she reached for her cell phone.

31

I t'd been a hellish couple weeks, with Owen in a foul mood and everyone at the station on his case to either snap out of it or fix the problem. Home wasn't any better, Opal tiptoeing around and Pearl shaking her head and muttering about how she couldn't wait to move into her own place.

He missed Hallie something awful, regretted that she'd cut him loose while he was still dumbfounded and reeling. The conversation they'd never finished was past due, but he'd needed the time to wrap his head around what had happened.

He was still grappling with that on his way to work Monday morning, but he knew one thing for sure. No matter how lousy he felt, for her sake he would stay away. The only thing to do now was stop by her place after work Wednesday and tie up any loose ends so they could both move on.

His mind made up and sick of his crappy attitude, he entered the department kitchen determined to suck it up and get on with his life.

Breakfast started well enough. Then Adam brought up her name.

"Hallie's down in Montrose City, Colorado, getting

info for an article on their fire department," he announced to the entire crew.

News to Owen, but she wasn't exactly texting or phoning him with updates. "Where'd you hear that?" he asked.

"Sam ran into Hallie at the grocery Saturday. Hallie was stocking up on dog food before she dropped her lab at her sister's. She flew down yesterday."

She must've gotten the okay for the series. "Good for her," Owen said.

She seemed to be doing a hell of a lot better than his sorry ass.

"According to Sam, she'll be down there through Wednesday, shadowing a firefighter like she did you."

The guy had better not make a pass at her. Owen started to get mad, but remembered he had no hold on her.

Things got busy and stayed that way, and he managed to put her and his unhappiness out of his mind for the rest of the day. He was managing okay Tuesday —until the mail arrived.

Miranda set an advance copy of the November Fire Prevention magazine on the dining table. Hallie's photo and a plug for her article on the Guff's Lake FD and her new series appeared on the cover.

Seeing her smiling face delivered a punch to Owen's gut. He read the article. Enthusiastic, energetic, and entertaining, it sounded so like her, he could almost hear her voice.

The hole in his chest widened and he forgot about his resolve to cheer up.

Something had to give, but for the life of him, he had no idea what.

~

A T DINNER OWEN'S crewmates steered clear of him. After the meal he and Hank shared cleanup duty. In no shape for chitchat, Owen did his part in silence. When they finished, Hank eyed him. "You're in a world of hurt, man. You need to talk to her."

Owen didn't explain that he'd already decided to say good-bye for good. He was in too much pain. He squeezed the bridge of his nose. "I need to get some air."

The nasty evening suited his mood. Pulling the hood of his jacket over his head, he hunched against the wind and rain and started around the block. He thought about Hank's words after their handball game a couple weeks earlier, that if Owen and Colleen belonged together they would never have thrown in the towel.

At the time he'd dismissed the idea. But maybe Hank had a point.

With new insight Owen recognized that he and Colleen had been polar opposites from the beginning. They'd entered into the marriage wanting different things but had never openly shared their deepest hopes and dreams. That made working out their problems impossible.

The marriage had been doomed from the beginning. A gust of wind whipped the hood off his head as if to say, It's about time.

Looking at it that way put a whole new spin on things. He knew what he wanted now. A life with Hallie. He wanted to commit to her and never waver.

He loved her.

He stopped in the middle of the sidewalk and

shook his head. How had he failed to realize this until now?

Damn. He was out of touch with his feelings.

He needed to get her back before it was too late.

Unless it already was.

Banishing the thought, Owen strode toward the station entrance. He'd never been good at laying his heart on the line. Since the divorce and Colleen's accusation that he was out of touch with his feelings, he'd grown even more reticent.

But if he didn't try, he wouldn't stand a chance.

32

Late Thursday afternoon, exhausted from traveling and the whirlwind trip to the Montrose City Fire Department, Hallie wheeled her suitcase to the pick-up area where Libby and Wilbur would meet her.

It hadn't snowed in Colorado, but after the freezing temperatures there, the cool Guff's Lake air felt downright warm. Hallie couldn't wait to see Wilbur and looked forward to sleeping in her own bed. Even if she was lonely and miserable.

But she wasn't going to think about Owen. That part of her life was behind her—or would be. Eventually. Despite the pain she was grateful to have fallen in love again. At least she knew she could. That counted for something.

Where was Libby? Shading her eyes against the slanting sun, Hallie searched for her sister's car in the line of idling vehicles.

She didn't see it, but she noticed Owen's Jag. He pulled to a stop, then exited the car. "Need a ride?"

Wary, she frowned. "Where's my sister?"

"I called and offered to pick you up instead." He stowed her luggage. "Let's go."

"I need to know why you're here."

"I owe you a conversation."

"After all this time? I'd rather not."

"We're going to talk." Drivers behind Owen's Jag honked impatiently. "Get in."

With a sigh, Hallie complied.

"Did you get what you needed in Montrose City?" Owen asked as he headed for the highway.

"Libby told you about that?"

Owen shook his head. "I heard about it from Adam who got it from Sam."

"They do live together and it is a small town. I filled a whole notebook and snapped a bunch of photos." Impatient to get the ball rolling, she angled Owen a look. "I thought you wanted to talk."

"Not in the car."

"But it'll take an hour to reach my house. Longer if we pick up Wilbur."

"He's staying at Libby's another night."

"I see." Beyond curious what Owen had to say, Hallie crossed her arms. "You can't just say you want to talk, then put me off." Her stomach growled.

Owen raised his eyebrows. "I'm not talking until you eat. The Loose Goose is about halfway between here and your place. We'll grab a bite and talk there."

Owen scrubbed the back of his neck and ushered Hallie into the Loose Goose. The small, cozy restaurant seemed as good a place as any to put his future in her hands. Scared witless, he rattled his keys and hoped to God he didn't screw this up.

Flashing a smile, a middle-aged waitress led them

to a booth and set menus on the table. Food was the last thing on his mind, but Hallie was hungry.

By the time they ordered, the dinner crowd had begun to trickle in, adding just enough noise to keep their conversation private.

Seated across from Hallie, he really looked at her for the first time since he'd picked her up. Beautiful as she was, she looked tired. No doubt she'd perk up once she ate.

"I looked up Montrose City," he said, making conversation. "It's a couple hundred miles from Denver with a population roughly the same as ours."

She nodded. "You did your homework. I flew into Denver and rented a car to get there."

"That's a long drive. What's the fire department like?"

"They have fewer firefighters than you, but the crews work the same back-to-back, twenty-four-hour shifts."

The food arrived. Hallie ate about half her baked chicken before she set down her fork. "Are you ever going to explain why you picked me up at the airport?"

It's now or never. Owen cleared his throat and began. "I told myself to stay away for your own good. It wasn't easy, but I managed. Then the advance copy of the November Fire Prevention magazine arrived at the station."

Hallie's shoulders slumped. "You didn't like the article."

"The opposite. It's great and sounds just like when you talk. I—" Do not blow this. To wet his suddenly dry throat Owen gulped the last of his water. "I'm not great at talking about my emotions, but bear with me." He laid his heart at her feet. "What happened last time we were together really messed with my head. I was ticked off at myself."

Hallie seemed puzzled. "Why would you be mad at yourself?"

"Because I sensed your growing feelings for me. I should have stopped what was happening while I could. But I wanted you too much, and you wanted me back. Once we started having sex the hunger kept growing until it was difficult to think about anything except making love with you.

"But that night... I looked into your face and knew how much you cared." He swallowed. "I never wanted to hurt you. If I'd pulled back from the get-go I never would have."

The same warm feelings softened her eyes now. "That's not your fault. You tried to warn me away."

Her forgiveness awed him and boosted his courage. "You aren't the only one with strong feelings, Hallie. I want you in my life, and I'm not talking about sex. Hell, I can't lie—I crave sex with you. But for now, spending time together is enough."

The waitress approached the table. Owen shook his head and she veered away.

"But you don't want to make a commitment," Hallie said.

"Thanks to my divorce I didn't think I could. I know better now. A lasting relationship is all about honest communication. If we talk through any worries or concerns, our relationship will strengthen and grow." He reached across the table and clasped her hands. "I'll commit to that. Will you?"

Hallie nodded, then sniffled. She pulled her hands from his to find a tissue in her purse. "Sorry I'm getting emotional."

"Don't ever apologize for openly showing your

feelings. It's one of the many things I love about you. I love every part of you, Hallie—even the stuff that drives me nuts."

"Like what?"

"Your impatience and bossiness."

"I'm not bossy. I... Wait. Did you just say—"

"That I love you? Yes, and if you'll have me, I'll devote the rest of my life showing you just how much."

Wiping her eye, she laughed, surprising and confusing him for the millionth time. She moved to his side of the booth, scooted close and cupped his face between her hands. "I love you, too. Saying those words to you feels wonderful."

His chest expanding, he tipped her chin up and kissed her. When he broke away she was flushed and dazed. And all his. He laced his fingers through hers.

Hallie sighed. "Where do we go from here, Owen?"

"Your place and straight to bed."

She smiled. "I like the way you think."

HOURS LATER, sated and relaxed in her double bed, Hallie snuggled closer to Owen. Life was good.

Except for one sticking point...

In the past she would have shied away from the subject, but she'd agreed to share any concerns with Owen. "Would you mind turning on the reading lamp?" she said. "We need to discuss something important."

Blinking in the light, she sat up. Owen followed her. "We aren't even close to thinking about marriage," she said.

He gave her a hooded look. "Is that a proposal?"

"It seems a little soon, don't you think? We need to

talk about our future, though. I know how much you want kids. So do I, but I want to make sure you understand that I'm not sure I want to attempt another pregnancy."

Owen nodded. "I haven't forgotten. I hope to God you'll change your mind. If you don't we'll look into adoption."

"You'd do that for me?"

"Hey, I love you."

Hallie felt like the luckiest woman in the world. "Love you back. Maybe I'll get counseling about it."

"Smart idea." He kissed the top of her head and shut off the light. They lay back down.

"You free tomorrow?" he asked, cupping her hip with his big, warm hand.

She snuggled closer. "I need to pick up Wilbur, and I should work. But I could take part of the day off. What do you have in mind?"

"I want you to meet my grandparents."

"I'd love to. Since you brought up the subject... What about Sunday dinner with my family? Are you up for that?"

"Sure—I can handle them. What are you grinning at?"

"It's pitch dark in here. How do you know I'm not scowling?"

"I feel your joy."

Awash in love, Hallie propped her head up on her elbow. "You're definitely in touch with your feelings."

"Thanks to you."

"You opened my heart, too. I never thought I could be this happy again. I can't wait to introduce you to Paige."

"Your BFF, right? Tell me when and where and I'll be there. Come back down here," he growled.

"Yes, sir." Hallie embraced the man she loved and their future with welcome arms.

THE END

THANK you for letting me share my stories with you!

There are 12 sexy firefighter books planned for the **Heroes of Rogue Valley: Calendar Guys**

IF YOU ENJOYED **MR. APRIL,** help others find this book by recommending it to your friends and by writing a review. If you would like to know when my next release is available and other fun stuff, sign up for my newsletter here: www.annroth.net

VISIT ME AT FACEBOOK FACEBOOK.COM/ANN-ROTHAUTHORPAGE

Follow me onTwitter @Ann_Roth

Email me at ann@annroth.net

Visit my website www.annroth.net

THANKS, and until next time,

Ann

PLEASE ENJOY this excerpt from **Mr. January:**

. . .

ADAM HEALEY WANTS a promotion at Guff's Lake Fire Department, which will finally earn him the respect of his dying father. Single mom Samantha Everett's deadbeat ex left her to fend for herself and she's struggling to support her young son. Neither Adam nor Samantha wants a relationship. But love has a way of surprising people ...

AT THE UNGODLY hour of five-forty-five a.m., Samantha Everett pulled into the delivery slot at Rosemary's Breakfast Nook. In the dark, the twin beams of the hatchback's headlights spotlighted the swirling snow. Well, it was early January in Rogue Valley.

"Please don't stick," she muttered under her breath, dreading the thought of putting on the tire chains.

Although so far, she hadn't needed them. When she'd moved to Guff's Lake six months earlier, locals had assured her that the usual winter temperatures tended to hover above freezing.

So different from the bone-chilling cold and frequent snowstorms in Enterprise.

"Look, Mom! Snow!" William chimed from the backseat.

At the age of five, he was delighted by almost everything—even at this hour. His joy was contagious, and Samantha's irritation dissipated like smoke. "I see it."

"Let me out." He unbuckled his car seat straps and bounced in anticipation for her to open the door.

Yawning—thanks to only five hours' sleep—Samantha exited the car. The building's perimeter lights cast long shadows across the nearly vacant concrete lot, a large area shared by several businesses. The few cars here now belonged to Rosemary, the cook, and wait staff. Rosemary's Breakfast Nook served the best breakfast in town, and snow or none, when the café opened at six, business would be brisk.

Despite the relative stillness, it was best to be safe. "Hold onto my coat," she directed.

Her itching-to-be-independent son grumbled but obeyed. Samantha opened the hatchback and jockeyed a dolly cart to the pavement. William helped her unfold it. Then she carefully loaded it with today's order—eight dozen still-warm cinnamon rolls, and six dozen each assorted muffins and scones. Her biggest order to date would net her more money than she'd ever earned as a baker in Enterprise.

Rosemary wouldn't pay her until a week from Friday, but Samantha had already divided and earmarked every penny. Groceries and other household expenses, bakery supplies, and the savings account for attorney fees.

To date, Jeff had ignored every one of the financial and custodial obligations spelled out in the divorce decree. Not one penny of child support or money for the debts he'd saddled her with, and not one request to see his son. Good riddance!

After all this time, Samantha doubted she'd ever hear from Jeff. She didn't need an attorney right now, but Betty Randall, her grandmotherly neighbor, believed that she did. Just in case. The woman had been so insistent Samantha had lost sleep over it. Mainly because Betty gave sound advice, unlike the unsolicited guidance from Samantha's parents.

William helped push the dolly toward the delivery entrance. As always, the door was unlocked for her, and easy to shoulder open and back through. Pausing inside the door, she brushed the snow off her son's parka and hat and then took care of her own coat.

The warmth, the fragrant aroma of freshly brewing coffee, and the haze from the sizzling vat of oil greeted her. A fragrant, smoky scent filled the air, and Samantha's mouth watered.

"Good morning," she greeted Rosemary and her longtime boyfriend and cook, José.

Round and perpetually cheerful, the forty-something restaurant owner greeted Samantha and William with her usual toothy smile. "Good morning." She winked at William. "How are you, sunshine?"

His small brow furrowed. "My name is William Tyler Everett Jones." Samantha had changed her last name back to Everett but had left her son's name intact.

From the time he'd first formed sentences, he'd insisted that everyone use his given name.

"I know that, darlin', but seeing you always makes me smile, and a true smile is as warm as the sunshine," Rosemary said. "Do you two have time for breakfast this morning?"

"Say yes, Mom." William gave Samantha the round-eyed, pleading look she'd never been able to resist.

Guff's Lake Bed & Breakfast, her only other paying client so far, didn't expect her until seven, and William's half-day kindergarten wouldn't start for several hours yet. She ought to use the time on housework—keeping the kitchen spotless was a constant chore.

But she really could use another cup of coffee and something to eat besides the bowl of cold cereal waiting for her at home.

"We'd love to have breakfast here," she said. "Can I put in an order for José's hash browns?"

José chuckled. "You bet. Bacon and eggs, too?"

"Yes, please."

"And cocoa?" William asked, going all round-eyed again.

Rosemary nodded. "I'll bring it with your breakfast."

As she filled a coffee mug for Samantha, Jana, one of the waitresses and Samantha's best friend, entered the kitchen through the restaurant's swinging doors.

"I thought I heard you in here. Can you believe it's snowing? I'll bet you love that, William. Let's get the case loaded."

Samantha wheeled the dolly to the counter out front, where bright walls and colorful posters added a homey, cheerful feel to the restaurant. She and William kept Jana company while she arranged Samantha's baked goods in the case and placed the printed "Treats by Samantha" sign in plain view. What didn't fit stayed in the delivery boxes for restocking the case until the restaurant closed at one.

Rosemary inspected the finished display with a satisfied nod. "You and William go on and make yourselves at home," she told Samantha. "I'll bring your food out shortly."

Samantha let her son choose where to sit. He led her to his favorite spot, a booth in front of the big picture window that faced the door. With the restaurant minutes from opening, Jana and the three other servers bustled around, seeing to last-minute details. Then one of the waitresses unlocked the door and welcomed in the morning's first customers.

Moments later, Rosemary delivered breakfast to Samantha and William. While Samantha enjoyed her food and coffee, her son chattered nonstop. During recess at Guff's Lake Elementary, the school he proudly called his own, he would have a snowball fight and build a snowman with Douglas and Harper, his two best friends.

Customers steadily streamed in to eat at the restaurant or collect their breakfast and morning coffee to go, some alone, others in groups. The almost twenty thousand Guff's Lake residents tended to be a friendly bunch, and even the people Samantha didn't recognize greeted her with nods and smiles.

Sipping a second cup of coffee and staring out the window with relief as the snow let up, she watched an orange 4Runner pull into the lot. A solid-looking male slid out of the driver's seat. Dressed in a leather bomber jacket, jeans, and a baseball cap, he wore a cast on one foot and a sling on his arm. A backpack swung from the other shoulder. Even with his arm injury and hobbling gait, he managed to move with a purposeful stride that for some reason reminded her of a big, sleek jungle cat. A tiger or a puma came to mind.

The sky had lightened a fraction, and between the approaching dawn and the perimeter lights, she easily made out his face.

And oh, what a face! The broad forehead, strong chin, and straight nose only added to his overall attractiveness. With a jolt of awareness, she recognized him. Adam Healey, aka Mr. January in the Guff's Lake Fire Department calendar that had come out last month, just in time for Christmas, as part of an ongoing fund-raising drive for the fire department's benefit fund.

The calendar featured twelve of the most gorgeous men Samantha had ever laid eyes on, and listed fascinating information, including height, weight, and marital status. She recalled that Adam was single.

Every female in town, along with a host of men

and all the local businesses, had purchased calendars. At Rosemary's Breakfast Nook, the calendar hung prominently in the display case, with Adam in his firefighter hat, grinning and shirtless under a deep blue sky. In the background, the snowy Siskiyou Mountains. Samantha glanced at it and blew out an admiring sigh.

Everyone knew that the guys from the Guff's Lake Fire Department hung out here, since the station a was mere two blocks away. Ordinarily Samantha came and went before any of them wandered in for coffee and breakfast. But today…

Adam must have sensed her staring at him, for his gaze met hers through the window. Embarrassed, she turned her attention to William.

"—read more *Charlotte's Web* to us today," he said, still chattering about his kindergarten class.

"That's such a great book," she replied.

The door opened, and a gust of cold air rushed in. But the man who shut it behind him sucked the chill right out of the room.

Adam's eyes were still riveted on her. She couldn't seem to tear her glance away, either. Up this close, his pale-blue eyes were even more striking than they were in the calendar photo. The color of the sky just before the sun rose.

It had been a while since a man turned her head, and she wasn't sure she liked that fluttery feeling of attraction. She'd moved here to escape Enterprise and the past and start fresh, and for the first time in more than three years, she was happy. Between taking care of William and supporting the two of them with her baked-goods business, socializing with friends and a weekly knitting class, she had filled her life to the brim. She didn't have time to look at a man, let alone date.

Or so she assured herself.

Ready to leave, she pushed to her feet and stacked her breakfast dishes to make cleanup easier for Jana. Her friend sashayed toward Adam with her hips swaying and a longing look on her face.

Jana was dating someone, but she wasn't blind. By the similar expressions the other waitresses wore, they were just as smitten. So were the other women in the café, who checked Adam out with approval.

"Hey there, Adam," Jana said with a flirty smile. "I didn't expect to see you this early in the morning. How are that wrist and ankle?"

"Getting better every day."

"Adam!" Rosemary bustled over with a grin on her face. "You're just in time to meet Samantha Everett, the bakery goddess behind Samantha's Treats, the goodies that bring you back every morning. Adam's a huge fan," she told Samantha.

"That's right. Hey." He touched the bill of his hat.

He was a big man, a good six inches taller than Samantha and powerfully built. Even wearing ankle boots that added two inches to her five-feet-six-inch height, she felt small.

"Hi," she answered, cupping her empty mug to her chest. As if it could deflect the mesmerizing warmth in his eyes.

"William, this is Adam Healey," Rosemary continued. "He's a firefighter."

"For real?" Her son looked starstruck.

"How you doing, sport?" Adam asked.

"My name is William Tyler Everett Jones."

"That's quite a mouthful. Mind if I call you sport?"

"Okay."

This was a first, and surprised Samantha.

Adam sniffed. "I smell smoke."

Right then, a waitress hurried out of the kitchen balancing several plates. Wisps of smoke followed her. The smoke alarm screeched, and people stopped eating.

"Everyone, clear out," Adam ordered in a booming voice. "Keep an eye on this." He handed his backpack to Samantha. On his way to the kitchen he pulled his arm from the sling, whipped out his phone and made a call.

"What's that noise? Where is he going, Mom?" William asked as he and Samantha donned their coats and headed toward the door.

"To see what set off the smoke detector."

"Why can't we go with him?"

"We don't want to get in the way. Besides, we need to get going." But she had Adam's backpack and she'd left her dolly behind the display case.

She would have handed the backpack to someone and come back later for the dolly, but her son dug in his heels. "I want to wait and see what happens," he said, his breath clouding in the cold.

The stubborn set of his jaw reminded her of Jeff when they were still married. Before he'd walked away from her and William, just days before her twenty-seventh birthday. The last time William had seen his father, he'd been all of twenty-six months old. Yet somehow, he'd picked up that stubborn look.

Getting him into the car without a battle wouldn't be easy, and Samantha didn't have the energy for an argument. With a sigh, she nodded and waited out front with the other restaurant patrons.

~

A BURNER HAD CAUGHT FIRE, and thick smoke rapidly filled the kitchen. Adam grabbed the fire extinguisher and went to work. In seconds, he had the flames out.

"Open the back door and get some fresh air in here," he directed.

Rosemary complied, and José swiped his brow. "That was close. I shouldn't have set that towel so close to the flames. It won't happen again."

Adam nodded. "Hang on while I call the station." He made the call then disconnected. "They're coming anyway. It's what we do."

His sprained wrist hurt like hell. Should've been more careful when he'd hefted the extinguisher. But his focus had been on putting out the fire before something really bad happened, and he'd forgotten to think about himself.

He started to massage it, winced, and slipped it back into the sling. With any luck, it would continue to mend, and he could start light duty next week. Eight hours a day, five days a week, doing filing and other administrative work. Not his job of choice. He preferred working a pair of back-to-back, twenty-four-hour shifts, fighting fires, or serving as a paramedic. Still, light duty beat sitting at home, twiddling his thumbs, and trying to study. The two weeks he'd just suffered through was more than enough time off.

"When did you last have a fire and life safety training refresher?" he asked Rosemary.

"I'm not sure. Maybe a year? Do you remember, José?"

"I'd say more like two."

This year, Nate was in charge of safety training, and Adam made a mental note to let him know to schedule something here. For all he knew, Nate might be on the engine today. Since Adam had been forced to take disability leave, he'd lost track of who did what this month.

"Let's clean up this mess and get back to work," Rosemary said.

José nodded. "I'll toss everything I was cooking, and start over."

"I'll let our customers know," Rosemary said. "Adam, how about coffee and a treat on the house?"

He couldn't argue with that. "A scone and an espresso sound good. Make it a double. I need the extra caffeine. This studying is a real bear."

Rosemary frowned. "What are you studying for?"

"The exam I need to pass so I can get promoted to lieutenant." That was the next rung up from senior firefighter and one rank below captain. Adam already knew a lot of what he needed for the job, but the class he'd enrolled in focused on management skills, which he didn't have. He'd made it more than halfway through the sixteen-week course, but there was still a lot to learn before the written test in late February. The class and the studying were rougher than he'd expected.

He returned to the restaurant and watched the diners file inside again.

In the midst of that, Rafe, Daniel, Hank, and Max strode in, just as Adam had known they would. Big men, decked out in fire gear.

"Like I told you, it's been handled," Adam greeted them.

"You know the drill," Adam's best bud, Rafe, replied.

Adam's crewmates tromped into the kitchen to make sure the fire was out and check for fire within the walls.

Samantha and her kid returned to their booth. She handed him his backpack.

"Mind if join you?" Adam asked.

When the little guy grinned, she shrugged. "Okay.

Adam slid in beside him, putting him across from Samantha. He'd heard about her—divorced, moved to Guff's Lake six months ago, house-sitting Lucy Marks's place while the older woman wintered in Palm Desert.

She was a looker—short black hair, long, wispy bangs, big eyes, and a sexy mouth that made him think of pleasure. But he didn't get involved with single mothers. He never had, mainly because most of them were looking for husbands. And judging by the relationships Adam had screwed up, he figured he'd make a lousy husband and father.

"Was it a big fire?" the boy asked. He had his mother's eyes.

"It could have been," Adam said. "But it's all good now."

William nodded somberly. "What happened to your arm and leg?"

Adam shrugged. "I hurt them fighting a fire." With his wrist still screaming, he figured he'd set himself back. That really teed him off, and not only because he wanted back on regular duty. Until he healed, he couldn't take the physical exam he needed to qualify for lieutenant.

Between the management class, the written and physical exams, and the interview, the whole process would take roughly four months. Time he couldn't afford to make up later, not if he wanted his father to see him promoted.

To finally make him proud. Adam wanted that just about more than he'd ever wanted anything.

His buds returned to the restaurant, stopping at the booth where Adam sat.

Every one of them looked Samantha over.

"Hello. I'm Rafe Donato." Flashing the twin dimples that had women falling all over him, Rafe shook her hand.

"This is Samantha and her son, William," Adam said by way of introduction. "I just met them myself. Samantha makes all that stuff in the front case."

"So you're the talent behind those scones. I'm Max Meier."

Max also shook her hand. Women said his brown eyes were soulful, and Samantha looked as if she bought that hook, line, and sinker.

Adam didn't like it, but what did he care? "These two other guys are Daniel and Hank."

Lanky Daniel grinned, and Hank, the station's newest and most solemn firefighter, nodded.

Each of them shook hands with her kid, who was all eyes.

Other diners came over to say hello. Adam didn't miss the looks women gave him and his buds. They were used to that.

A moment later, Rafe checked his watch. "We're a little over an hour until the end of our second shift. We should go."

The crew's back-to-back shifts started at eight a.m. on Mondays and ended at eight a.m. on Wednesdays, when another crew took over.

"Good to meet you, William. Samantha." Rafe nodded to Rosemary and the waitresses. "I'll see you ladies for breakfast shortly."

As they filed out, Adam swore he heard collective female sighs.

Although Samantha seemed immune to his crewmates' charms. Adam wasn't about to examine why he felt relieved.

"We should leave now, too," Samantha said. "We still have another delivery to make, and then William needs to get ready for school."

Already standing, the boy cupped his groin and danced from foot to foot. "Mom, I gotta pee."

Samantha gave Adam a *Kids, what can you do?* look and then slid quickly from the booth. "Hurry, before you have an accident."

"I don't wanna use the girls' bathroom."

"Well, I can't go into the men's."

"I'll take him," Adam offered.

Unsure whether she should trust this man she'd just met with her son, Samantha hesitated. "That isn't necessary."

"I gotta go right now," William insisted.

"He's a good guy," Janna added from a nearby table, where she was pouring coffee.

Samantha relaxed. Anyway, there was no time to argue. Adam ferried her son toward the men's room. "Sit tight, Sam," he said over his shoulder. "We'll be right back."

SAM. Adam had called her Sam. Samantha sat back in the booth and sighed. She didn't go by the shortened version of her name anymore, hadn't since high school. Even her parents called her Samantha.

She kind of liked hearing it again on Adam's lips. Not that she was interested in him. She wasn't, she assured herself.

By the time he brought her son back, she was up

and waiting with her coat on and holding out William's.

"Thanks, Adam." She helped her son into his parka.

"No prob. Be good, sport."

"I will."

"Hey, I'll be back at work next week. If you ever want to visit the fire station, give me a call and I'll show you two around." Adam wrote his cell number on the back of his card.

"Really?" William looked as if it was Christmas morning.

Samantha preferred to steer clear of the firefighter she was attracted to, but she couldn't bear to disappoint her son. "We just might take you up on that."

A tour to please William, and that would be that. As they headed toward the car, she pushed the firefighter from her thoughts.

PLEASE ENJOY this excerpt from **Mr. February:**

FIREFIGHTER RAFE DONATO is well aware that loving a woman can destroy a man. He will never trust any female with his heart. Jillian Metzger is a talented potter whose biological clock is ticking. Ready to fall in love, get married and start a family, Jillian wants what Rafe cannot give.

"COME BACK HERE, POOH!" Jillian Metzger shouted as she sprinted across the uneven field adjacent to the cottage.

The Border collie had the gall to bark joyfully and

skip over rocks and tree roots at a clip Jillian couldn't begin to keep up with.

To make matters worse, it started to rain. She hadn't taken the time to grab an umbrella, let alone a jacket—she'd simply darted out of the studio in hot pursuit. Not wise, considering temperatures in early March in Rogue Valley tended to be on the south side of chilly.

If and when she managed to catch Pooh, she was going to let her freeloading brother have it. Why couldn't JR keep an eye on his own dog? Because he'd gone out with Chelsea, frittering his day away when he should have been looking for a job.

Pooh was a good fifty yards ahead now, and Jillian quickly losing steam. She was on the verge of collapsing in exhaustion when the dog finally skidded to a stop. Tail wagging, Pooh changed course, trotting toward a man and woman standing slightly uphill, under a big umbrella. What were they doing here in the boonies on a rainy Wednesday morning?

Jillian lurched to a halt to catch her breath and pull herself together before they noticed her. A futile effort, given that she was a sodden mess. Leaning against the trunk of a lofty tree heavy with leaf buds, she tucked her dripping hair behind her ears with icy fingers.

She couldn't tear her gaze from them. What a striking couple. The dark-haired male, muscled and at least six feet tall, wore jeans, a light-blue sports shirt, and a black windbreaker that hugged his broad shoulders. His companion, with her shiny, stylish haircut and designer suit, stood close beside him under the umbrella.

Something about the guy seemed vaguely familiar, but before Jillian could place him, Pooh did the unthinkable—raced forward, jumped up, and planted her muddy paws on his powerful thigh.

"Get down, Pooh!" Jillian cried, pushing away from the trees and running again.

The big man didn't seem all that upset. He patted the dog and then brushed the mud off his jeans, which were neatly pressed, as was his shirt. Clutching the umbrella in both hands, his horrified companion quickly stepped out of reach.

The second his dark gaze met Jillian's, she recognized him. What red-blooded woman could forget those mesmerizing eyes, the strong jaw, and the slight hollows of his cheeks? She was about to come face-to-face with Rafe Donato, aka Mr. February in the Guff's Lake Fire Department calendar.

The calendar, part of the ongoing fund-raising drive for the department's benefit fund, had been released right before Christmas and featured twelve of the most gorgeous firefighters...

Drop-dead, movie-star-handsome Rafe looked even better in person than his photo—if that was even possible. Jillian's heart lifted in an appreciative sigh.

The calendar included certain important facts about each firefighter, stats any woman with a pulse would want to know. According to the details Jillian recalled—and with a calendar hanging on the wall in her studio, she was quite familiar with them—Rafe was single. At least he had been when the calendar was printed. By the intimate look from his lady friend, his status had changed.

"I'm sorry about Pooh," she apologized. "She's supposed to stay in the yard. Instead, the little scamp dug under the fence and lit out."

When Pooh had made her escape, Jillian had been in her pottery studio, creating pieces for one of her retail customers and for the Rogue Valley Arts Festival, which was in March. If she hadn't decided to stretch her back and wander to the window, she wouldn't have noticed until the dog was long gone.

"My dog used to do the same thing."

Rafe flashed a smile, revealing dimples—holy cow, dimples—and extended his arm.

"Rafe Donato."

Wishing she'd dressed in something other than raggedy work clothes, Jillian wiped her palms on her threadbare, damp jeans before she shook his huge hand. His firm, warm grip engulfed her cold fingers, and his chocolate-brown eyes fixed intently on her.

Her knees wobbled. She glanced away. As attractive as Rafe was, she refused to go all weak and fluttery. He was already taken.

Even if he hadn't been, the ramrod straight posture, military-short hair, meticulously pressed shirt and jeans, and polished black boots screamed order and control. This was the kind of man who made life miserable for everyone around him. At eighteen, she'd left home to get away from that. She would never go back.

Pooh licked Jillian's hand. "Bad girl," she said, but the dog's innocent expression was hard to resist.

Rafe's girlfriend cleared her throat. "I'm Sonia Kaye, Rafe's architect." She started to extend her hand, but, after giving Jillian a quick once-over, offered her card and a perfunctory smile instead. "I should go, Rafe. I've seen enough for now, and I took plenty of photos. I'll be in touch."

"Let me walk you to your car." He held up a finger, signaling Jillian to wait.

Pooh wanted to follow the couple, but Jillian caught hold of her collar. "You're not going anywhere."

The dog put wet-dog smell on a whole new level, and Jillian grimaced. "You need a bath."

With JR and Chelsea out, who knew where—they certainly hadn't said good-bye or left a note, but then, they never did—she would likely be the one doing the honors.

Rafe and his architect girlfriend moved in tandem up a gently sloping hill, toward the two expensive sedans parked on a dirt patch some distance away—one, a silver Mercedes, the other a gleaming navy convertible BMW.

Which belonged to him? The sleek BMW, Jillian guessed. It looked cleaner and somehow suited him.

Yep, the convertible was his. Rafe held the umbrella over Sonia's head while she climbed into a silver Mercedes. After flashing a flirty smile, she drove away, her tires churning up mud.

Rafe tromped back to Jillian. "Where do you and Pooh live?"

"Not far. On the other side of the field."

He nodded. "Cy Jackson's property."

"How do you know the name of my landlord?"

"I just bought the two-acre plot you're standing on, and I know everything about this area. Your cottage isn't more than a third of a mile from here, an easy walk, but this driving rain can make even a short distance seem like a long way. How about a lift?"

The offer surprised her. "We couldn't possibly. We're both wet and muddy, and Pooh stinks something terrible." She held her nose.

Rafe didn't argue with her. "You don't even have an umbrella. I do. I also happen to have a spare leash in the trunk of my car. Let me grab it, and I'll walk you and Pooh home."

Jillian was tall, the top of her head almost level with Rafe's nose. That put her at about five-foot-ten. Long-limbed and slender, she could pass for a runway model—at least from what Rafe imagined. In baggy, wet clothes and dirty sneakers, he couldn't tell.

Her wet, shoulder-length blonde hair lay plastered to her head. Rafe remembered how cold her hand had felt in his. Any minute, her teeth would start to chatter.

"Here," he said, setting the umbrella down to shrug out of his lined windbreaker. "Put this on."

"But I'm a dirty mess."

"You're also freezing cold." He helped her into it then picked up the umbrella and held it over them. "Don't worry, it's washable. Zip up."

She did. The thing swam on her, which was kind of cute.

"How long have you lived on Cy's property?" he asked.

"For almost a year. Last month, I signed a lease for another year."

"We'll be neighbors, then—once I get my house built."

When not at the Guff's Lake Fire Department, Rafe spent his time managing his rental properties. He also kept an eye out for fixer-uppers, which he enjoyed remodeling and selling. With the combined income he earned, he'd finally saved enough to build his dream home without emptying his bank account.

"Your own custom place? Lucky you. Sonia must be so excited."

"Because I hired her to design the house?"

"That and because you're a couple."

He laughed. "We're not together."

"Oh." Jillian looked surprised. "I assumed... You know."

"Getting romantically involved with my architect could be risky."

"Because if it didn't work out, you'd still need her help."

That and because as much as he liked women, and he liked them a lot, he didn't trust a single one enough to live with. Which wasn't quite true—he trusted his paternal grandma and a handful of female teachers from grade school and high school. But he preferred living alone. "Yeah."

Jillian nodded then angled her head. "You're a firefighter, right?"

"You've seen the calendar."

She blushed, adding much-needed color to her pale skin. "I have."

She had a generous mouth and fine, delicate features. "There's something on your chin," he noted, nodding at the gray glob stuck on the underside. The same stuff stained the cuff of her oversize sweatshirt. "And on your sleeve."

She touched the spot on her chin and rubbed at it, laughing self-consciously. "It's clay. I'm a potter."

"Ah. You do that full-time?"

"Yes. I sell to a couple of stores in the area an online. I'm also working on pieces for the Rogue Valley Arts Festival in Medford next month. Until recently, I also taught at the Artist Cooperative on the south side of town."

"You don't teach there anymore?"

"The school closed up shop last month. I'm getting ready to offer classes in my home studio."

"I never figured that little house with room for a studio."

"Actually, I use the outbuilding behind the cottage. With heat, electricity, and a skylight, it's perfect. I think it was originally designed as a workshop for household projects. I got permission from Cy to turn it into my pottery studio. My kiln is behind the building."

Rafe wondered how she made ends meet selling pottery and teaching classes. Having spent the first ten years of his life with his mom, whose sales from herbal concoctions and tie-dye T-shirts had often left them both hungry and moving in a hurry to escape eviction for non-payment of rent, he preferred a steady job with a regular paycheck, and money in the bank.

As they neared the cottage, Pooh woofed and strained at her leash.

"*Now* you want to get home," Jillian quipped. Under her breath, she added, "You'll change your tune when you realize you're about to get a bath."

Rafe chuckled, caught himself, and frowned. He wouldn't let this woman charm him.

Tibetan prayer flags were strung across the eaves over the porch. That and the aging VW van parked behind the hatchback in the gravel driveway reminded him of the years he'd lived with his mom.

Jillian frowned. "It's about time JR got back."

Rafe figured JR was her boyfriend. He wasn't about to ask—didn't want to know, but the words slipped out. "Who's JR?"

"My brother," she grumbled. "Thanks for walking me home, and for loaning me your jacket."

His unwitting gaze dropped to her plump, inviting

lips. Jerking his attention to the jacket, he held out his hand for it.

"Let me clean it first. I'm happy to drop it off at the fire station later."

The guys were sure to razz him. He shrugged. "Sure. I won't be in again until Monday."

"Then you're a part-time firefighter?"

He shook his head. "I work Mondays and Tuesdays, two back-to-back, twenty-four-hour shifts. That's forty-eight hours a week, with five days off in between."

"Your days off sound nice, but isn't it dangerous, working such long hours with no break?"

"We each have a place to bunk at night, so I usually get some sleep. Even on busy nights, I manage all right. After eleven years, I'd better." Ready to leave, he gestured at the cottage. "Stay dry."

He turned away and strode back toward his property.

PLEASE ENJOY this excerpt from **Mr. March:**

FIREFIGHTER GUS VIGGIO needs to convince the stubborn great aunt who raised him and recently suffered a stroke to give up the house that has become too much for her. When she refuses, Gus enlists help from her flamboyant hairstylist, Wanda Lippman. The two women get along well, and Gus's great aunt just might listen to Wanda. Wanda and Gus have both been hurt by love, and neither is ready to venture back into those dangerous waters anytime soon. But sometimes the heart knows best...

. . .

THE SECOND GUS VIGGIO offered his great aunt Polly a boost into his Jeep Cherokee, she shook her cane and fixed him with that stubborn *I'm not a helpless old lady yet* look that warned him to back off. God help him if he attempted to buckle her in.

Hands shoved into his jeans pockets, he stood by the open passenger door. Just in case. She wasn't as strong as she used to be, and those arthritic hands made even fastening the seatbelt difficult.

While he waited, he squinted against the sun, bright but not strong enough to take the chill out of the April morning. Almost overnight, spring had sprung in the Rogue Valley. Here in Guff's Lake, grass, shrubs and flowers, dormant through the winter, had made up for lost time and grown by leaps and bounds.

"My yard is mess," Aunt Polly lamented.

Once an avid gardener, she could no longer handle yard work. Gus had taken over the job, with occasional help from his father. "Dad and I will stop by and take care of it this weekend."

Maintaining the large front and back yards took a big chunk of time, but Gus didn't mind. He loved Aunt Polly dearly. When his mom had left, his great aunt had invited him and his dad to move in and had raised Gus as her own.

Years ago, they'd decided to dispense with the "great" label, respectively shortening their names to "Aunt Polly" and "nephew." Not that "aunt" cut it, either. She was more a mother and grandmother rolled into one. He would do anything for her. Anything.

Buckled in at last, Aunt Polly folded her hands in her lap. "What are we waiting for?" she said with an impish look. "Let's boogie."

He grinned at her word choice. "You're in a good mood today."

"On such a beautiful morning, how could I not be?" She slipped a pair of sunglasses over her bifocals. "Besides, it isn't every day my favorite nephew and two of his fellow firefighters take me to lunch at Ellen's."

The stuffy restaurant wasn't at the top of Gus's go-to list, but his aunt loved eating there, and his buds enjoyed her company, so they tolerated the place.

"Your *only* nephew," he reminded her, pulling on his Ray-Bans.

"If I had a dozen, you'd still be my favorite."

"Not favorite enough to take my advice."

Her lips thinned. "Don't you dare start in on me about my living arrangements, Augusto Frances Viggio. I'm perfectly able to take care of myself, and you know it."

The use of Gus's full name meant she was seriously irritated, but didn't change the fact he disagreed with her.

Insisting on independence, she lived alone in her big, old house. No amount of reasoning or cajoling had convinced her to downsize and move into an apartment in a retirement community.

She did allow him to chauffeur her around, thanks to a stroke ten months ago that had put an end to her driving. Gus didn't mind shuttling her where she needed to go—when he could. Between him and his dad, they managed.

"If and when I decide to leave, I promise to let you know," she added. "But don't hold your breath." Raising her chin, she changed the subject. "As I was saying, you are my favorite nephew. Who else can I rely on to take me to my weekly hair appointment with Wanda?"

Gus tabled the conversation about moving—for the moment. "No problem."

Tommie's Hair and Nails was an easy ten-minute drive from Aunt Polly's house. "I need to schedule an inspection at Tommie's. May as well set that up today."

"For the safety project?"

"That's the one."

Gus had been tasked with checking fire and smoke alarms in every commercial and multi-dwelling residential structure as well as updating computer diagrams with the safest routes into and out of each. Important information that was posted in every building for both civilians and emergency responders to use during emergencies.

Gathering and collating all that data in the town of almost twenty-thousand people was taking more time than Gus had estimated. When he'd started ten weeks earlier, he'd promised the captain a finish date of early August. As tight as the deadline now seemed, he intended to deliver, even if it meant working off the clock.

No longer cross with him, Aunt Polly tilted her lips into a fond smile. "Not just anyone is strong and smart enough to be a firefighter. I'm so proud of you."

Gus's chest expanded. Not one for big displays of emotion, he gave a modest shrug.

"I can't wait to tell Wanda about lunch today," Aunt Polly said. "She'll be all ears. She's a darling, that one."

Darling wasn't the word that came to mind when Gus thought of Wanda Lipmann, who looked to be in her late twenties. He never knew what to expect when he saw her. Short and curvy, she wore her clothes bright and tight, and she changed her hairstyle and color a couple times a month. Talk about unsettling.

They hadn't spoken much, except to say hi and bye when he brought Aunt Polly in and picked her up.

His aunt cast him a sly look. "If you'd get to know Wanda, you'd realize how special she is."

Gus narrowed his eyes. "Stop right there. You are not fixing me up—now or ever."

"But it's been almost a year since your breakup with Delores."

"Denise," he corrected. "I'm way over her."

For sure. After she'd pressured him one too many times to get married, he'd decided to break up with her. Then Aunt Polly had had her stroke. "Trust me, if I had time, I'd be dating. I happen to have a lot on my plate."

Between working at the Guff's Lake Fire Department, looking after Aunt Polly, and running his one-man classic car restoration business, Gus was overbooked.

Not that he wanted to give up any of his responsibilities. His car business relaxed him and felt more like play. Currently, he was restoring a 1965 classic Lincoln. His customer had agreed to pay top dollar, with a bonus if he finished in time for the classic car show in mid-May.

Whipping off her sunglasses, Aunt Polly gave him the no-nonsense look that had always worked during her librarian days, her still-bright eyes serious behind the bifocals. "At thirty-two, you're not getting any younger."

"Don't hold back."

"Have I ever? It's time you found a wife and settled down. That should be your priority, but because it isn't, you need help. Mine."

She'd been after him to get married since the day he turned thirty, nagging him with a dogged determination that wouldn't quit.

Gus narrowed his eyes a fraction. "Stop."

"I will not." She sniffed. "Come October, I'll be eighty. I've earned the right to speak my mind."

"Like that's anything new. You know I'm not against marriage, but there's no guarantee it'll happen."

"Pish posh," Aunt Polly said. "Of course it will."

His parents had split up when he was seven, but he had good little-kid memories. Settling down and having two or three children appealed to him. But to date, every one of his serious relationships had gone south.

In matters of the heart, he'd begun to think he was just like his father. This apple hadn't fallen far from the tree.

Gus pulled onto Brewster Street, home to a dozen small businesses on the west side of town. Tommie's Hair and Nails salon was always buzzing, mostly with women, and judging by the number of cars parked in the salon lot, this morning was no different.

"This is a wash-and-trim appointment. I'll be done in about thirty minutes," his aunt said as opened the passenger door for her. "Since you need to schedule that inspection, you may as well wait inside."

Having just come off forty-eight hours—two back-to-back shifts—at the Guff's Lake Fire Department, with a couple calls in the dead of night, Gus planned to grab some quick Z's in the Jeep while Aunt Polly had her hair done. He'd deliver her to Wanda, schedule the inspection, then make a beeline for the Jeep.

Refusing his arm, she relied on her cane. In the sunlight, the sparkly Tommie's Hair and Nails sign on the door glittered. Gus ushered his aunt inside and removed his shades.

The half-dozen or so females in the process of

manicures and haircuts stopped chattering and stared at him.

Every week he brought Aunt Polly here, but you'd think they'd never seen him in the salon. Maybe it was his size. Bigger than many men, he'd grown used to curious looks. Lately, more than usual, thanks to the firefighter calendar.

Feeling awkward, he nodded at Carol Sue, who had about ten years on him.

"Nice to see you, Polly. Hi there, Gus," she said, batting her lashes at him.

"Hey," he replied, courteous but not too friendly.

A flirt and a gossip, Carol Sue lived to spread rumors. Here in Guff's Lake, information spread faster than a forest fire in summer. Gus preferred to stay out of her stories.

"Who do I talk to about scheduling a salon inspection?" he asked.

"That would be either Tommie or Wanda. Tommie's out just now, but Wanda is here. I'll let her know you and Polly have arrived. Help yourselves to coffee. The one with the orange band is the decaf you want, Polly. The other is leaded. Enjoy." She sashayed off.

Gus got Aunt Polly settled on the sofa and brought her a decaf with sugar and creamer. He filled a Styrofoam cup with the leaded stuff and sat in a chair. A few sips in, the "Employees Only" door at the rear of the salon opened. Wanda and two stylists stepped inside.

Sticking close to the door, all three glanced his way and whispered. God knew what they were saying. As long as it didn't go on too long, Gus didn't care.

He took another few sips of coffee before Wanda started forward.

~

POLLY BECKER RANKED among Wanda's favorite customers. She wasn't so comfortable with Polly's great nephew.

At six foot four and two hundred thirty pounds—details everyone who owned a Guff's Lake Fire Department calendar knew—Gus, aka Mr. March, was a strikingly handsome man. All solid muscle, he was built more like a super-fit linebacker than a firefighter. The piercing green eyes and short, light-brown hair with a hint of red didn't hurt, either. Looking at him, a woman would have to be dead not to have heart palpitations.

The calendar, sold to raise money for the station's benefit fund, had turned Gus and the eleven men featured into local celebrities.

Nadia, a stylist and close friend Wanda had been chatting with in back, elbowed her. "He always drops Polly off and leaves," she said in a low voice. "Carol Sue says he wants to talk to you today. I wonder why?"

"What does it matter, as long as I'm in the same room as him?" murmured Rochelle, Wanda's second closest friend. She worked from noon to closing on Wednesdays, but had come in early to accommodate a customer. She fanned herself. "He's even more gorgeous in person."

In place of his usual T-shirt, jeans and weathered leather jacket, he'd switched it up in a pressed blue shirt, dark pants and polished black oxfords. He looked good in dress clothes, but he looked equally fine in casuals.

"Maybe I'll move my schedule around and start working early on Wednesdays." Rochelle gave Wanda a sideways glance. "Unless you have dibs on him?"

Currently, both Rochelle and Nadia were single and in the market for a boyfriend. Wanda frowned. "Tommie depends on you to work late Tuesdays and Wednesdays. And don't forget, I'm taking a break from men."

Her friends shared a look. "You say that every time you go through a breakup," Nadia pointed out. "Until some cute guy asks you out. Then you're off and running again."

"After I've turned down every guy who asked me out the past six-and-a-half months? If that isn't serious, I don't know what is."

She refused to date until she figured out how to win and hold a man's love with more than good sex. She had the sex part down but not the rest, and her heart had been broken more times than she could count.

The latest split with Larry had hurt almost as much as losing Wayne ten years earlier. In hindsight, she realized much of the pain stemmed from her seriously wounded pride. She'd tried her best to keep Larry interested but had failed. Yet again. She didn't think she could survive one more breakup.

"To clarify," Rochelle said, "you're not interested in Gus Viggio."

"Right."

Even if a mere glance at the man caused a spike in her pulse rate, he'd never given her more than a brief greeting and a cursory glance. A good thing, too. Otherwise, she might be tempted to forget she'd sworn off guys, proving her friends right.

"Polly's waiting for me," she said. "And apparently so is Gus."

Curious as she was about what he could possibly want, she paused and fluffed her layered, purple-streaked, blond hair—a far cry from its dull-brown natural color. She strutted forward, her teal, three-inch ankle boots clicking smartly across the tile floor. The walk had taken years to perfect.

As she drew closer, Gus pushed to his feet. His great aunt had raised him right.

"Morning, Polly," Wanda said, with a warm smile.

The older woman beamed. "I like your hair, Wanda. Those purple streaks are fun. And what a snazzy outfit."

"Thanks." Wanda smoothed her short-sleeve, lavender tee over her hips. Even with the three extra inches of the ankle boots, she was only five feet six. She tilted her head back a little to greet the firefighter. "Hello, Gus."

He nodded, his expression impossible to read, and gave her a once-over from her head to the hint of cleavage, courtesy of the low scoop neck, where his gaze lingered a beat longer than an uninterested man's should have. Then past her flared, teal skirt to her black leggings.

Pride surged through her. As with her walk, the cutting-edge hairstyles and clothing had never been natural to her. Neither was being bubbly and talkative. But wanting to be noticed and liked by men, even though she'd temporarily sworn off them, she'd adjusted. Her efforts had paid off. Getting a date when she wanted one was never a problem, and both male and female customers kept coming back.

Proving Cindy right, for once.

"I'm told you're the one to see about scheduling a safety inspection," he said, his deep, sexy voice vibrating through her.

Safety inspection—of course. A little part of her had assumed he wanted information of the personal kind. What a relief he didn't. Or so she assured herself. Yet something inside her deflated a fraction. "I'm the one, all right."

"Do you have any time Monday?"

"We're closed that day, but I guess that'd work."

"If you're closed, who'll let me in?"

"Either Tommie or me."

Likely Wanda. Tommie had just turned sixty-five and decided to retire at the end of September. Wanda wanted to buy the business and the building—provided she saved up enough for the down-payment necessary to secure a loan. Although she still needed a fair chunk of change, she'd assured Tommie that when the time came, she would have the required funds.

The past few months, Tommie had been teaching her the ins and outs of running the salon, and slowly giving Wanda more responsibility.

"Your aunt should be ready to go in about a half hour," she told Gus. "You can pick her up then."

"He's going to wait here today." Polly showered him with a fond grin. "Then he's taking me to lunch at Ellen's."

No wonder he'd dressed up. "Lucky you." Wanda sighed.

She'd always wanted to try the upscale restaurant, but not one of her boyfriends had ever taken her there. "Have a seat in the waiting area, Gus. I'll bring her to you when we finish. Come on, Polly, let's make you gorgeous."

She offered her arm, but Polly rebuffed her. Thanks to her shoes, Wanda stood some two inches over the woman. She also moved a lot quicker. She slowed way down, and they made their way to her station across the way.

Or tried.

Polly dug in her heels and waved her cane at Gus. "Aren't you coming with us?"

"My station is small, and there's no place for you to sit," Wanda pointed out. "You'll be more comfortable in the waiting area."

So would she. If he hovered around, she wouldn't be able to relax.

"Nonsense. He'll bring a seat with him," Polly insisted. "I want him to see what you do."

"Aunt Polly..."

Wanda didn't understand Gus's warning look."

Lips compressed, Polly turned away from his gaze.

While he returned to the waiting area to grab a chair, Wanda helped her into the salon chair. She fastened a large plastic smock around Polly's neck, gently tipped her back to wash her hair, and wondered what her customer was up to.

ALSO BY ANN ROTH

Ann Roth Classics

A Place to Belong

Father of the Year

Another Life

My Sisters

Dunlin Shores

Book 1 Just the Way You Are

Book 2 Wedding Bell Blues

Book 3 Falling for Mr. Wrong

Book 4: A Special Kind of Love

Firefighters

Book 1 Mr. January

Book 2 Mr. February

Book 3 Mr. March

Book 4: Mr. April

Book 5: Mr. May

Book 6: Mr. June

Book 7: Mr. July

Book 8: Mr. August

Book 9: Mr. September

Book 10: Mr. December

Halo Island

Book 1 All I Want for Christmas

ABOUT THE AUTHOR

Ann Roth is an award-winning author of 40-plus contemporary romance and women's fiction novels, as well as novellas and numerous short stories. Her first novel was published in 2000 by Harlequin Special Edition and was nominated by *Romantic Times* as best first book. Ann lives with the love of her life in the Greater Seattle area and enjoys creating flawed characters and putting them in challenging situations that help them grow and ultimately find love— whether or not they're looking for it.

Find out about new releases!
Sign up for my newsletter

Or visit my website www.annroth.net